STILL WATERS

An Outport Newfoundland Murder Mystery

CHRIS RYAN

Dedication

Still Waters touches on the subject of suicide. I would like to dedicate this book to anyone who is suffering from a mental health issue. More specifically, for anyone who is suffering and has not reached out for help. There is help available. If you're not comfortable speaking to a health professional, reach out to a family member, a friend or a learneth person in your circle or community. I have suffered from mental health problems since my preteen years. I was finally diagnosed in 2001, as being Bipolar, along with Attention Deficit Hyperactivity Disorder{adhd} and Obsessive Compulsive Disorder{ocd}. I have a grade six education. I do not blame my teachers for this. Teachers were not trained back in my era to pick up on students with learning disabilities and mental health problems. Learning in a classroom environment was too fast for me to grasp. When I was medicated, I became a

STILL WATERS

Chapter 1

When Dr. Patricia Delmont, Chicago psychologist, landed at St. John's International Airport on a chilly January morning, Dr. Bill Welsh, a tall, thin-faced greying professor of psychology from Memorial University of Newfoundland, was there to meet her. On the drive to the university to meet with the team assembled to work with Delmont, Welsh explained what it was like living in rural Newfoundland. The province, he told her, had the highest incidence of alcoholism in Canada. And that, he said, likely had a lot to do with the problem she had been brought north to investigate: an unusual spate of suicides in a rural area.

When the two entered the conference room at the university, two people were seated at a table. Both stood to introduce themselves, Dr. Mary White, a short, white-haired woman, taught at the medical faculty, as did Dr. Gregory

Small, a large, bald man. White explained why the team was small: the project was a trial run for Newfoundland.

After everyone was seated, White said, "As chair of this committee, I anticipate that we will meet at least once a month, more often if needed. As you all know, Dr. Delmont will live in the town of Setback, but will stay temporarily at the local hotel in Black Tree until a house is found for her in Setback."

Black Tree was an urban town that serviced thirty communities on the northeast coast. It had all the usual amenities, plus a cottage hospital. White told Delmont that there was a problem with Black Tree's cottage hospital and the hospital in Gander: neither had a psychiatrist on staff or even on call. If a resident of the northeast coast needed emergency psychiatric care, they had to be transported to the capital city, St. John's, either in an ambulance or by the Royal Canadian Mounted Police. The RCMP policed most rural Newfoundland communities.

Delmont felt a prick of dismay. She knew this would cause problems with patients in her field of work. If she counselled a patient and that patient ended up in hospital, she needed to continue to treat them until they were well enough to return home. She explained this to the committee. White told her that Dr. Shandal, the head of psychiatry at the Health Sciences Centre, the largest hospital in the city, would meet with them the next morning to discuss this and other issues. White also gave Delmont a short history of the closure of the leading industry in Newfoundland the previous summer, the cod fishery. Codfish, she told her, was the reason the English first became interested in the island, back in the fifteenth century. The closure had ripped apart the cultural fabric. The fact that a small place like Setback, population 359, having had five suicides seemingly related to loss of livelihood since the fishery ended, bode ill for the rest of the province. The government was worried about these numbers, and afraid that Setback was only the beginning. They wanted to find out what the people needed in terms of psychiatric care.

Delmont looked up from her file folder. "Why is there so much alcoholism and drug addiction on an island with such a small population? It can't all be related to the closure of the fishery. My research indicates that alcohol has been a problem in Newfoundland going back many generations."

Welsh spoke up. "There are many studies linking island populations with seasonal industries to problems with alcoholism, and it's apparently a more significant issue in smaller populations with extended downtime. People drink as a pastime to counter boredom, and before they realize it, most have an issue with alcohol and/or recreational drugs. And that pretty much sums up this province. But the closure of the cod fishery has greatly exacerbated what was already a problem, and this is a great cause of concern to us. I have some more material here for you, on the fishery and the culture and the mental health and addictions, that should flesh out what you already know.

"Now, I'm sure Dr. Delmont is tired from her flight and would like to get to her hotel, so, lady and gents, we'll see you tomorrow at ten. Cheers."

On the way to the Holiday Inn, Welsh told Delmont that he would be travelling with her to Black Tree, and help her settle in. "It's over three hundred kilometres away. We might have a small population, but the circumference of the island is nearly 109,000 kilometres, bigger than the Netherlands, which has a population of seventeen million."

"Why is the population so small, then?" Delmont looked taken aback.

"Well, it's a rocky place off the beaten track, so agriculture and industry have never flourished here, just the fishery and forestry. The young tend to leave for greener fields, Ontario and Alberta, usually. They can make the big bucks there. Some of them come back later, which is why there is a high percentage of elderly people here."

Welsh took three large suitcases from the trunk at the hotel, put them on a trolley and wheeled them inside.

Delmont thanked Welsh and told him she'd see him in the morning. As she watched him leave the hotel lobby, she thought how friendly her colleagues were. This was her first trip to Canada east of Montreal, but a colleague of hers from the University of Chicago had told her about the legendary hospitality of Newfoundlanders, when he had travelled here to visit the Viking settlement at L'Anse aux Meadows on the Northern Peninsula. She would like to visit it herself if it wasn't too far away from Setback. According to what Welsh had said about distances in the province, it might be halfway to the moon.

The following morning when Delmont arrived at the conference room, the only person there was Welsh. He greeted her warmly and asked if she would like a coffee.

"That would be nice."

When Welsh returned with the coffee, he asked her how her first night on the Rock had been.

"The Rock?"

"Oh, sorry. We call it that, sometimes. Big chunk of granite out in the North Atlantic that it is."

Delmont smiled. "I hadn't come across that reference."

"The island is a cornucopia of linguistic gold, Dr. Delmont-"

"Tish, please."

"Tish - which is not always easy to interpret, especially around the bay."

"Which bay?"

"Any bay. Anywhere in rural Newfoundland, that's what 'around the bay' means. If you're not from St. John's, you're a bayman. Or woman. You're in for a rude awakening when you get outside of St. John's. Newfoundland has at least twenty different dialects, both Irish and English and quasi-English with some Scottish thrown into the mix. Every bay sounds different. If we left here and drove south for an hour and a half, we would reach the towns of Ferryland and Renews on the Southern Shore. If you stopped and spoke to the older men, you would think you were in Belfast or Dublin."

"Interesting. I guess I'm not in Kansas anymore."

Welsh chuckled. "Oh no, and you're not in Chicago, either. Although I believe there's a large Irish demographic there as well."

"It's the largest demographic in Chicago, actually."

"Well, top of the mornin' to you, then."

Delmont laughed. "Oh no, not me. My people are from Austria, you know, the *Sound of Music*. Edelweiss. Beer. The Anschluss."

Welsh grinned. She was an attractive woman, Dr. Delmont. And not just because of her grey eyes, blonde hair, and slim figure. She was smart and engaging.

Dr. White arrived, and then Dr. Shandal, and, finally, Dr. Small.

White asked Shandal if he would like to speak first.

"Sure. Dr. Delmont, I will start by saying you are in a unique part of the world. Outside of St. John's and a few other urban areas we have in this province, the people who live in the bays and harbours along our coastlines are not like those in the rest of North America. They speak differently, act differently and live differently."

Delmont smiled and said, "Bill told me that."

"The inhabitants of this island have been here almost 500 years. Newfoundland's maritime culture is gastronomically blessed with fish. The people in rural Newfoundland have always loved to eat fish, mostly because they had no access to any other meat besides salt beef. They eat every part of the cod fish, and often consume the flesh with the skin still attached. The tongue of the cod is considered a delicacy, also the bladder and roe – sounds and britches, the locals call them. They even eat the flesh of the jawbone, known as sculps. Lobster and crab make up part of the local diet as well. In the summer, a tiny fish called capelin comes to the beaches to spawn, and they are considered a delicacy, both here and in Japan. They are processed here in the fish plants and sent to Asia. The females are prized for their roe; the males are used mostly for fertilizer or dog food."

"Interesting," said Delmont. *Not*, she thought. What was his point – that people were killing themselves here because they couldn't get enough fish to eat?

"But that's enough about our dialect, diet and way of life. We believe what is happening is connected to the closure of the cod fishery. The average age of the victims of suicide is between thirty-five to forty-five. Most people in rural Newfoundland are not as educated as those in urban areas. A substantial percentage of the outport population does not finish high school. Historically, they dropped out of school, knowing they had a full-time or at least a seasonal job in their communities. These people are now in a no man's land. With little education and no secondary training, they are trapped in a small, lifeless world. And it seems some are taking a sad, quick way out of the situation they have been put in.

"We must produce a plan to reassure these people that there is a future beyond the cod fishery and a future beyond rural Newfoundland. We must reassure these people that the federal government will be there for them in the years to come until the fishery recovers, be it three, five or even ten years down the road. We hope, Dr. Delmont, you can produce a mental health template we can use in other communities. And that we will be able to present the provincial government with a plan."

"Would anyone like to add anything?" asked White.

Small spoke up. "I'd like to add a few things. First, I would like to thank Dr. Delmont for coming to our province with her well-known, sterling credentials." He nodded his head and smiled at the American psychologist.

"Tish," Delmont said, smiling back.

"Understanding and healing this social issue will not be easy. Every time I go home to visit my family, there's more trouble brewing." Small was the only person on the team from rural Newfoundland. He had grown up in Sop's Arm, White Bay, on the eastern side of the Great Northern Peninsula, his family one of a few hundred in the community.

"Another social issue is a mass exodus of residents out of the province. This team has met with several provincial cabinet ministers, and obviously, the government is worried about its young population migrating to the mainland. Newfoundland cannot afford to lose them. Our population is small, and it is ageing. Our economy will tank."

Delmont sighed, not too audibly, she hoped. "Well, this all sounds pretty dire, and possibly above my pay grade. It may even be above God's pay grade, by the sounds of it. But I – we – will do what we can, within the confines of our discipline. It will be a monumental task, however, and will take a year or two at least, I believe. This is not the first time in history, of course, that primary industries have collapsed and left people high and dry. Detroit's automotive sector took a severe downturn in the seventies, and one of Norway's fisheries collapsed in the sixties. We can learn from those and other cases."

"Premier Wells and his cabinet have assured us that neither time nor money is an issue, Tish. But they would like to see some results as soon as possible, of course.

Anything else?" queried White.

Welsh told the committee he and Delmont would leave for Black Tree and Setback in the morning.

"Fine, Bill. There will be a press release issued tomorrow, about the project and Dr. Delmont's role in it. Thanks for coming, everyone – see you soon."

Outside, the sun had broken through the clouds, but it provided only a weak, winter light. Delmont shivered and made a mental note to pick up some warmer clothes. She told Welsh she needed to spend some time in the university library, and afterwards do some shopping. He told her he'd pick her up the next morning at eight. The drive to Black Tree would take three and a half hours.

The following day brought a grim sky and intermittent snowflakes. Delmont was waiting in front of the hotel at eight o'clock, in a bright red, thick wool jacket when Welsh pulled up. He put her suitcase in the trunk as she settled herself in the front seat of the car.

When Welsh got in, Delmont said, "I love the smell of the sea, that tangy salt smell."

"It's a good thing you do, girl," Welsh said. "You'll be smelling it every day now. Actually, it's not the smell of salt, you know, salt actually has no odour. It's the smell of decaying marine life." He took his eyes off the road and quickly smiled at her. "As with so many romantic things, there's often a dark underbelly."

They stopped for lunch at the Irving gas station in Clarenville. Welsh ordered fried cod and recommended it to Delmont. "It's fried with bits of pork fat, which we call scrunchions. You can ask them to leave the scrunchions out."

"No, that's okay. I like to try local stuff, and I've got a thing for pork. All the pork schnitzel of my youth, I guess. The only thing I ever turned down was chicken feet. That was in the Caribbean."

"Chicken feet? Christ, those guys must be even poorer than we used to be."

As they took the turnoff for the coast, Welsh told Delmont she would be shocked to see the places where people lived, the little settlements that seemed to cling to the rocky outcrops.

"I'm always excited to see a different part of the world. I've never been this far north before. Can't wait to take out the camera."

"Actually, we're not that far north. St. John's is on the same latitude as Paris, but you'd never know it. It's cold here because of the Labrador Current, which comes right down the coast from the Arctic Ocean."

Eventually, they pulled into the hotel parking lot in Black Tree, both tired from the long drive. They agreed to meet for dinner at five in the hotel restaurant. At four-thirty, Welsh called Delmont and asked if she would like to meet for a drink in the bar.

"Sure. Just have to brush my teeth and comb my hair, and then I'll be right down."

Welsh was standing at the bar when Delmont walked in. She looked different from the woman who had driven from St. John's with him. He suspected she must have had a nap and a bath and the outfit she was wearing was sharp looking.

"What would you like to drink?"

"Vermouth, please. On the rocks, with a twist of lemon."

He headed towards one of the booths with his scotch and water, and she followed him with her vermouth.

Welsh wanted to pick the American's brain. He also needed to see what kind of person he would be working with on this project. After their second drink, Delmont became more talkative. She told Welsh she hadn't married yet but supposed she would someday. And perhaps there would be a kid or two. He told her he had remarried five years ago, to a cardiologist who worked at the Health Sciences Centre. His first wife had been unable to have children, and he and his second wife had decided not to have them.

"I guess it's six of one and half dozen of the other: you don't know what you're missing without them, but you know you're probably missing something. But Kerry and I live to travel, and kids would put a crimp in that, at least for a while."

At five-thirty, they headed for the restaurant. Delmont asked Welsh if the restaurant would have fish with scrunchions.

"Most likely. Rural Newfoundlanders eat cod at least three or four times a week, dried, stuffed and baked, broiled, deep-fried and stewed."

"Well, I guess I'll get around to each of them in time. I don't eat much meat because of the health risks, but fish is pretty healthy. I'll have to extend my runs if I'm going to eat it with pork fat, though. I don't see much in the way of salads on the menu."

"No, you won't see much in the way of salads in these parts. The standard Newfoundland vegetables are carrots, potatoes, cabbage, and turnip. Vegetables that are easily cultivated in this climate here, and which could be stored in root cellars over the winter."

By the time the meal was over, Welsh had had five glasses of wine. Delmont was uneasy. They had saddled her with an alcoholic, by the looks of it. She hoped he wasn't suicidal or stupid, although she could go it alone if she had to. She'd often had to.

Chapter 2

After breakfast the next day, Welsh and Delmont headed for Setback—a thirty-minute drive from Black Tree. The council building in which they would be working was situated between a Roman Catholic church and the public wharf. It looked like a relatively new modern building. But it was shabby, with peeling paint on the eaves, and the thick wooden door to the main entrance looked like it was refurbished from a schooner long gone.

"Most of these small towns don't have much of a budget, Tish. Money is always tight for infrastructure maintenance and repairs. These small towns survive on operating grants from the provincial government because there's not a lot of tax money coming in. They have to keep taxes low because most of their people are seasonal workers."

"Yes, I came across that in my research. Oh well, as long

as my desk doesn't go through the floor, I don't care." She pulled her collar up around her ears. The wind was blowing from the land, where it had apparently had lunch on a glacier.

The town clerk was waiting for them inside the door of the building. Welsh made the introductions.

"Sally Osmond, I'm Bill Welsh. We met when I came here to see about renting the offices a few months ago. This is Dr. Delmont, who's come all the way from Chicago to work and to help the people of Setback and Newfoundland."

Sally held out her hand. "Pleased to meet you," she said.

Delmont felt the soft, warm hand in hers. How lovely the girl was, small and dark, with exotic big brown eyes. She looked like a North American Indian from the Great Plains. She had small hips and breasts, she was tall and well proportioned. Long dark hair, a good cut for her face. She reminded Delmont a bit of the singer Rita Coolidge. There had been native tribes in Newfoundland once, Delmont knew. Perhaps this girl was one of their descendants?

Sally Osmond showed them the meeting room and then took them to their offices, telling them on the way that she would be their go-to person within the town. She was the intermediary between the public, the mayor and council, and the Royal Canadian Mounted Police. The latter had an office in the back of the council building.

"We managed to squeeze a few bucks out of the budget to get some pictures for your walls - hope you both like them.

They're the same as the ones in Dr. Welsh's office. We got a deal on them from a gallery in Corner Brook."

Delmont looked at the three prints, a deer, an even larger deer with strange horns – that must be a moose – and an odd, cartoonish-looking bird. She could live with them; at least they wouldn't make any noise. She suddenly missed her miniature dachshund, Bella, whom she often took to the office with her back in Chicago. Bella was living the life of Riley with Delmont's sister now, and her two kids. She probably didn't miss her one bit.

"They're lovely, Sally – thanks so much."

She was rewarded with a smile from Sally that went straight to her heart.

"Moose were brought here in 1878, two that year and four in 1904. Now there's thousands of them. Mind when yer drivin' at night you don't run into one! Also, if you want, I can get you some bottled moose to try – my aunt makes the best bottled moose you ever had."

"I'm sure she does," Delmont said, and smiled noncommittedly. She had never tasted bottled moose and had no intentions of doing so. Wild animals should be out decorating the landscape, not sitting in jars on a shelf. "Can we three meet tomorrow morning Sally, or are you busy then?"

"No, I'm fine with that."

Again, that smile. Be careful, Delmont told herself.

After the clerk left, Welsh turned to Delmont and said,

"Sally seems like a nice girl. I hear she's got a small child, a daughter she's bringing up on her own. She's been here for a couple of years and has a good reputation. A smart cookie, apparently. Has a diploma in business administration and loves to read, according to my sources. Although listening to her, you wouldn't think it."

"Why, I could listen to that child all day, Bill. She sounds like something out of an English folktale."

Welsh rolled his eyes and left the room.

The following morning at nine, Welsh, Delmont and Osmond met in Delmont's office.

"So, Sally, what are you hearing around town, what have things been like since the fishery shut down? Are things very different here now?"

This time Sally didn't smile. "Oh, it's a sad old place these days, it is so. People are in a flat spin, drinkin' all the time. The RCMP says impaired charges are at the highest rates they have ever seen around here. And then there's people doin' away with themselves."

The clerk's voice had dropped so low Delmont could barely hear her.

"People are frightened, they want to know when things are goin' to get better. People are broken - not broken in the financial sense, but their spirits are broken. We have couples livin' here that have spent thirty and forty years workin' in the fish plant and now they are doin' nothin', just sittin' home livin' off government handouts. Newfoundlanders are proud and hard-workin' people. Government handouts is not their way of life."

The American felt pity invade her. She had a desire to hold the young clerk in her arms and comfort her. Well, maybe she and her colleagues could make a difference to Sally and her people, although she had her doubts. Delmont wasn't sure her contract was to do with window dressing on the part of the Newfoundland government. Time would tell. Maybe.

"Sally, do you have a computer in your office?"

"No, Dr. –"

"Tish"

"Tish – no; I don't know how to use one."

"It's not that hard, Sally – you'd pick it up in no time. I'll help you. Bill, can you get in touch with whoever requisitions government computers? We need three of them, of course."

"I think that's already being processed, but I'll check on it for you. So, what are your plans for Setback? Initially, anyway?"

"Well, on Monday, I'd like you both to help me get the word out to the displaced fish plant workers and fishermen and fisherwomen of Setback and its neighbouring communities that the provincial government is offering counselling. A chance to talk about what's happened and how they feel about it, and what comes next. Over the weekend,

I'm going to do some more reading – history, settlement patterns, sociology. All that good stuff. I've done a lot of reading before I came here, but more can't hurt." She smiled at her two colleagues and pushed a piece of escaped hair back behind her ear.

"Also, Bill, I need to know when to expect a car and a place to live."

"I'll get on that as well, Tish. I think that's already in the works – at least, it should be. But you know government bureaucracy."

"Not firsthand, but I've heard."

A week later, Delmont entered Osmond's office, grinning, and waving an envelope with a letter sticking out of it.

"Well, Sally – it's official – I'm now a resident of Setback. I've got a place here somewhere. You'll have to show me where, because apparently there are no numbers on the houses."

"Oh, Tish, that's grand news! Whereabouts is this house?"

"It says it's the former Squires house on South Side Point Road."

"You take a right turn as soon as you come into Setback from the south. The Squires' place used to be a Christmas tree farm in the eighties. It's a beautiful old house. Definitely the nicest house and the nicest grounds in the town. And private, not another house for a kilometre or more. It's at the end of a dirt road, on a cliff overlookin' the ocean. It even got a beach, Maggoty Cove beach, just beyond the property. You can watch the whales from the deck, and there'll be lots of seagulls, gannets and turrs flyin' around."

"What's a turr?"

"It's a kind of seabird. We eat them sometimes, although they stink somethin' awful when you cook them, and they're right oily. But turr gravy is considered the best gravy in Newfoundland."

Delmont wrinkled her nose. Greasy turrs and bottled moose. At least Setback had a couple of hamburger joints and a pizza parlour. She thought wistfully of the Thai restaurant in her Chicago neighbourhood, and then resolutely put it out of her mind. She would pick up cooking supplies in Black Tree. They must stock chicken, pork, lean meat and some vegetables.

"I can help you move in, if you want, Tish. I got a flair for decoratin', especially old places."

Tish thought of the prints in her office and inwardly shuddered. "That's really nice of you Sally, but it's fully furnished. You can come over and have a glass of wine with me if you like after I get settled."

"I'd love to, Tish. I like red wine; I drink a bottle or two on the weekends."

Christ, was everyone on this island an alcoholic? "Great, Sally. Well, I've got to get back to work. See you later."

Delmont stopped in the corridor and looked out of a window. The landscape was breathtaking with snow, but so was Chicago's this time of year. It was much bleaker here, though, without the city hustle and bustle, and the buildings. Even Sally's smile wasn't a match for the barrenness of this landscape. She suddenly felt a million miles from anywhere.

The public notice of counselling had gone out a week ago on the local cable station that covered the area north and south for fifty kilometres, and to the unemployment office in Black Tree. It stated that counselling would be available to all former plant workers and fishermen and fisherwomen displaced by the closure of the fishery. Dr. Patricia Delmont from Chicago, an expert in employment loss and its effect on people's mental health, would be providing free counselling sessions, under the federal government's Northern Cod and Adjustment and Recovery Program (NCARP). All were welcome.

The notice was broadcast on a Monday, and by the following Monday, five people had called to enquire about counselling: two women, former fish plant workers; two men who also worked in the plant; and one inshore fisherman.

Delmont's first patient was Toby Green, a fish plant

worker. He was a massive man, fifty years old, rugged, lined, and looking like he had native blood. Delmont wondered whether he was related to Sally. Not that she was going to ask; this was strictly business. She felt as though she'd seen him somewhere before, and then realized he looked like the actor Will Sampson, the guy in *One Flew Over the Cuckoo's Nest*.

After they shook hands, Delmont told him to sit in whichever chair he preferred. She sat in a hardbacked rocker near the door, which she had closed behind him. "Mr. Green, welcome. Before we begin, I want you to know that everything you say to me in this room will be held in the utmost confidence. The only time I must break that confidence is if I have reason to believe you intend to harm yourself or someone else or abuse a child."

Green gripped the arms of his chair and stared at her so hard and so malevolently she wondered if he was going to leap up and come for her.

"As if I ever, Dr. Delmont, would ever, even for one second, consider harmin' one hair of a little child's head, so help me God, I hope you would turn me in. I hope God himself would strike me dead, so I do. I only ever give me youngsters a smack growin' up when they needed one, the same for the wife. And the only creatures I ever kills is fish and chickens and pigs and rabbits and turrs, and the scattered moose - without a license. I suppose you're goin' to tell the RCMP about the moose, are you?"

"No, Mr. Green, your secret is safe with me."

Mr. Green visibly relaxed "Well, that's grand, girl. I'll remember to send you over a nice piece of moose the next time I gets one. Or some bottled moose, how would you like that? The wife -"

"I'm afraid I'm not allowed to accept gifts from patients, Mr. Green. Guess I'll just have to miss out. Now, Mr. Green, can you tell me why you came here today?"

"Well, it's like this, Doctor. I'm half out of me mind with the plant shuttin' down. I was only ever a weekend drinker before, got ossified every Friday and Saturday night down to the club, but now I'm startin' to drink every day. To be honest with you, the wife made me come here. She said if I don't get the drinkin' under control, she's goin' up the cove to live with her sister. And as much as we fights, I'd miss her some bad, I would."

"Well, Mr. Green, even if your wife made you come to see me, it was the right thing to do. When people have problems, it's a good idea to talk to someone who isn't a friend or a family member about them, and it's particularly helpful to talk to a professional like myself because I have a lot of experience with people and their problems.

"Would you like to tell me a little about yourself, Mr. Green? How you grew up, what your life was like before the fishery closed? Would you be comfortable doing that, do you think?"

"Yes, sure, I don't mind. Well, missus – Doctor – me life, I suppose, was just like anyone else's in these parts. There were ten of us growin' up – eleven, but Joe drowned when he was small. Mother took on somethin' awful about that, but she got over it pretty quick - had to, no time for lyin' around snottin' and bawlin' when you got a husband and ten other kids to look after. My father was a fisherman, and I went on the boat with him when I was thirteen. Had to quit school in the sixth grade to help him out. He couldn't afford to pay an extra crew member when he had a big strappin' son at home who could do the work. Besides, I never liked school much – draggin' two chunks of wood a mile every day for the pot-bellied school stove, and then sittin' around on me arse – sorry, Doctor – in that hard seat all day. Well, I got married and had six youngsters of me own, got me own boat eventually, and then give that up to go work in the fish plant when they built it. Youngsters all grown and gone now, up to the mainland. Only a couple of the girls are still in Setback. They married fishermen, and they're not havin' an easy time of it right now, as you may well imagine."

Delmont thought she'd like a drink herself right about now. Jesus, what a life. No wonder these people drank. "Well, Mr. Green, that's quite a story. It's too bad that your life has been shaken up through no fault of your own. I'd like to know, however, if you ever felt this way before the fishery closure. Have you ever felt really sad for a prolonged length of time, for no particular reason? Unable to cope, get out of bed?"

"No, nothin' like that. Never had time to be sad – or happy. You works all day, goes home, eats whatever the missus puts in front of you, watches some TV and falls into bed. Now, if you ever were feelin' a bit blue – and I'm not sayin' I ever have, mind you – well, maybe a scattered time or two – a nip or two of rum would straighten you right out. We drank a bit on the boat; kept the chill off. Had a swally or two at the fish plant some days, or nights, if we were on night shift. But this is different. It's no good, no good at all."

Delmont sighed internally. It sounded like the entire culture was depressive and probably had been since day one, sometime back in the 1400s. Suicide numbers had been rising in the province for a decade, although no one really knew why. It was likely they would continue to rise, although there was always a chance something could be done to slow it down. Alcohol had always been a problem here, and the abuse that went with it. Mr. Green hit his kids and wife only when they "needed" it. She had a sudden longing to be standing on Lake Shore Drive back home, looking out at Lake Michigan with a big vibrant city at her back and a cup of steaming cappuccino in her hand.

"Mr. Green, I'm going to suggest that you try to stay away from alcohol for at least two weeks, at which time you'll come back to see me, and we'll discuss your progress, stay away as much as you can from people who drink, and keep as busy as you can. Surely your wife could use some help?"

Green looked as if she'd slapped him in the face. "Yeah, like I'm goin' to go around tied to *her* apron strings."

Chauvinist pig, like a lot of men. "Well, go for walks, go

fishing, chop some wood – whatever makes you feel better. And if you're still not doing any better in two weeks, we'll have to consider medication."

"Nerve pills?" Green made a face and crossed his arms.

Delmont made a face of her own. "Mr. Green, if I told you, you had diabetes and had to take insulin, you would accept it. The brain is only another organ, like the pancreas. If it's not working properly, it needs help. Two weeks from now, all right?"

Her next patient was scheduled for two in the afternoon. She asked Sally if she was interested in a walk while on her lunch break.

"Oh, yes, I would. If I'd known you were a walker, I'd have worn somethin' to work that was more practical to go walkin' in than these shoes." Sally stuck a foot around her desk, black patent leather flats, with shiny soles. "I usually go for a walk after I get home before the sitter leaves. Pregnancy and a desk job, well, I got to move when I can, keep the weight off."

"You don't look like you've ever had a problem with weight," Delmont said, allowing her eyes to casually run down the length of Sally's body.

"Only for a while, after I had Bette. I was as big as a whale when I was carryin' her."

Delmont wondered what had happened to the child's father. Was he still in the community, or had he ever even been here? Perhaps Bette was a souvenir of Sally's stint at school in

St. John's. She supposed she'd find out in time, over a drink of wine or vermouth on that deck in her new old house.

Delmont's next client was a fisherman, Bill Grant, thirty years of age. He shook hands with Delmont and introduced himself.

"Miss – I means Doctor – you're the best-lookin' Yank I ever seen, men included."

Delmont gave him a curt nod but then smiled. "Thank you, Mr. Grant, but it sounds like you haven't spent a lot of time in the States."

Grant laughed, a deep, pleasant sound. He was a handsome man. Tall, with dark, somewhat weathered skin. More native blood, or all that exposure to the sun and sea air? He was well dressed for a fisherman. Or at least her idea of one. But he had bags under his bloodshot eyes and his fingers were nicotine stained. A sour smell came from his mouth. A soul in trouble, this one, by the looks of it. But weren't they all?

Delmont explained to Grant what patient confidentiality covered and what it didn't.

"Well, Doctor, the only thing I does that's illegal is applyin' for a moose license for Grey River and shootin' one in over the ridge behind Setback."

"Yes, there seems to be a lot of illegal game hunting in this area. But that's your business, not mine. Now, Mr. Grant, would you like to tell me why you've come to see me today?"

Grant suddenly lost his congenial air. "My best friend, Jack, Skellington, killed himself six weeks ago, and it's killin' me. We were best buddies since elementary school, known him nearly all my life. I can't sleep, and I'm drinkin' from daylight to dark most days. Smokin' three or four packs of cigarettes. I mean, we knew the closin' down of the fishery was goin' to be hard on us, but I never knew it would be this bad. Christ." Grant stopped talking and pulled out a pack of smokes. "Do you mind, Doctor?"

Delmont reached into a drawer in her desk, pulled out an ashtray and set it in front of him. Then she got up and opened the window a few inches. As much as she disliked the smell of smoke, it was an occupational hazard she'd gotten used to.

Grant lit up and expelled a cloud of smoke and a deep sigh. "What got to me the most is that he never confided in me. We were drinkin' the night he did it, on the beer all day in his shed. As content as two pigs in shit in a sty. Singin', playin' guitars and the accordion. We did some talkin' about what was goin' to happen now that the fishery was gone, and God knows when it was ever comin' back. And this is what's the hardest: when Jack left the shed that night, he did it. He hugged me and told me he loved me before he left. He never, ever in his life told me he loved me, and if I hadn't been so fuckin' drunk and stupid - excuse the language, sweetheart - as I said, if I hadn't been drunk, I would have picked up on it. He went home and blew his head off with a shotgun in his shed. If either of my brothers had done it, I don't believe I would be havin' as a hard time as I'm havin'. I loves me brothers, but Jack and I, well, we were soul brothers, that's the only way I can put it. I was in shock for a while and when that wore off, I thought I'd start to feel better. But every day it's gettin' harder."

"Mr. Grant –"

"Bill."

"Bill, I think I can help you get through this, but you'll have to cooperate with me."

"Doctor, I'm that desperate I'd crawl on my hands and knees to Fogo if I thought it would help. What do you want me to do?"

"First, you need to stop drinking. You are obviously depressed, and alcohol is absolutely the worst thing in the world for depression. But I need to know if there is any possibility you were an alcoholic before your friend died because if you were, quitting drinking cold turkey could kill you. Alcohol is the only drug that is capable of killing an addict who quits." She looked at him with what she hoped was a sympathetic but firm expression.

"No, Dr. Delmont, I only ever drank on the weekends before, maybe one night durin' the week. Nothin' serious. Never had the DTs or nothin'."

"Okay. We'll give it a try, but if you do get the DTs or have any other kind of severe reaction to stopping drinking, physical or mental, I want you to promise me that you will call an ambulance, if when you go to the cottage hospital, I'll be there as soon as they notify me. I'll contact them and arrange that today, that they must get in touch with me if you get in trouble. In the meantime, I'm going to get in touch with your GP here and recommend that she or he write you a prescription for a sedative, to help you sleep, and an antidepressant. The antidepressant can take up to three to four weeks to work. In the meantime, stay away from people who drink, and try to keep active. Get outside as much as you can. And come back to see me in a week from today, at the same time. If you feel you need to see me before then, call and I'll fit you in. If that's not possible, I'll send you to Dr. Shandal in St. John's. He's a Psychiatrist and a colleague of mine, with an excellent reputation. He's a very nice man. Easy to talk to."

Do you have any support at home, anyone you feel comfortable talking to about your feelings?"

"Yes, my wife, Margaret. She's my rock, but I don't know how long she's goin' to keep puttin' up with me in this state. Her patience is runnin' thin. Not that she had any patience to begin with."

"So, you're ready to start on the road back to health, Bill?"

"I guess I got no other choice. If not, I'm afraid I'll end up like Jack."

"We must change your way of thinking. There's help available, and we will do everything in our power to help you. You're not the first person I've seen in this shape for the same reason. You *will* get better, in time. But you have to think positive, that it will happen."

As she ushered him through the door, Grant suddenly put his arms around her and hung on like a drowning man. This was not an uncommon occurrence in her field. She gently disengaged him and shook his hand. "See you next week. Call if you need to. Sally Osmond is taking my calls for me,"

Grant smiled, the first easy smile she'd seen from him. "Oh, Sally, she's a grand girl. Too bad she got mixed up with that son of a bitch, and Bette's a fine child."

Delmont and Osmond ate lunch together on Friday. Delmont had ordered a pizza, cheese and mushrooms and green pepper for her, and all the fixings for Sally. She told the clerk that some extra furniture for her new place would be arriving from St. John's the following day.

"That's excitin', Tish. I really would like to help you settle in, rearrange what's already there, maybe, and fit in the new stuff."

"I have a condo in Chicago, and a decorator did it up for me."

"What's a condo, Tish? Sound like a bird I've seen on one of them nature programs."

"That's a condor, Sally. A condo is just a fancy name for an apartment, but you buy them instead of rent them."

Chapter 3

On Saturday morning, Delmont packed up and left the hotel. It was time to move into the old Squires' homestead.

When Tish got to the end of the long driveway by the sea, she stopped the car and drew a deep breath: the place was beautiful. A big Victorian, with dormer windows and gingerbread trim. It was surrounded by trees, aspen, maple and birch. She got out and walked to the front door, inhaling the mix of whatever trees gave off and the smell of decaying marine life that constituted that ocean fragrance.

A delivery truck appeared before she managed to get her key in the lock. There were only a few pieces – a new bed, a desk, an ergonomic chair, and a scattering of smaller objects that had caught her fancy in St. John's. And some fitness equipment, of course. She was a long way from a gym.

While the men hauled the furniture inside, she explored

her new living space, wondering if the Newfoundland
government prized her skills so highly that they were willing
to pay what must be a high rent for this huge heritage house,
or had they gotten the cheapest place in town, a white elephant
that none of the locals wanted. It didn't matter; she would like
living here, she could feel someone was knocking on the door.
Delmont was startled, and then she remembered: Sally had
promised to come to the house to help her settle in. She wasn't
really in the mood for company, she liked being alone in this
large, quiet space after suffering the ordeal of hotel living for
weeks. Oh well, an hour or two with Sally wouldn't hurt.

When she opened the door, Sally was standing on the
crumbling wooden steps with a bottle of wine in one hand and
a pot of flowers in the other.

"Why Sally, how lovely! You didn't have to do that.
Chrysanthemums, my favourite – and my mother's."

"Welcome to Setback, Tish." Sally's smile was positively
beatific. Tish figured Sally was happy to be out of that mouldy
old office building. She, Tish, was, anyway.

"Come in, let me show you around."

"I can't wait to walk through this house. I've always been
in awe of it, it's so beautiful and has so much character."

Just like you, my girl, thought Delmont. She took Sally
through the old house, room by room, Sally made delighted
noises over the fireplace, the ten-foot ceilings, panelled walls,
crown moldings, and the vivid colours someone had used to
spruce up the plaster walls.

"I think I'll set up a little gym in the lavender room, Sally. You can come use it if you want. Actually, I'd like to give you a key to the house. It's always better if someone you know has a key to your house in case you lose your own. And I have a tendency to lose keys."

"I've never been to a gym, Tish. Don't know the first thing about any of that stuff, that equipment they have in them places."

Tish grinned. "Oh, it's not that complicated. I could show you – you'd pick it up fast enough."

Sally, I'm not really in the mood to drag furniture around today. Would you like to hang out for a while, have a cup of coffee? I saw some in one of the cupboards, but you'd have to have it black because I haven't picked up any supplies yet. There's tea there too."

"Sure, Tish. Black tea's fine by me."

They sat down at an old wooden table in the substantial kitchen. Osmond remembered a half box of donuts she'd left in the backseat of her car a couple of days before and ran out to get them. Tish allowed herself two, with a mental note to run two extra kilometres that afternoon.

"So, Sally, have you always lived in Setback?"

"Oh, yes, Tish, all my life. Except for that time, I went to the trades college in St. John's to get my diploma. I never liked the city much. Bunch of snobs those townies are, I can tell you that. And I missed my mom and my dad, and my brother. And Rex."

To Delmont's astonishment, the girl suddenly burst out crying, and it wasn't gentle weeping either. She sounded like she was giving her last gasps on earth. Frantically, Delmont looked around for the box of tissues she knew wasn't there.

"Sally, Sally, what is it?"

"Oh, Tish, I'm so sorry, I never meant to cry, I just . . ." But the sentence became lost in another bout of sobs, and Osmond bent over the table. Delmont got up and went around to where her guest sat and put her arms around the slim, warm body. The girl relaxed after a minute or two and sat up and wiped her eyes on her sleeve. Delmont sat back down and waited.

"Sally, you don't have to explain, you know. It's okay. Would you like me to top up your tea?"

"Yes, please. No, I'll tell you what's wrong, that's if you want to hear it. You don't have to. I know you hear sad stuff all day long in your job, and it's the weekend, and . . .."

"But you're my friend, Sally. Of course, I want to know what's troubling you. It's not the same thing as my job at all."

Sally's smile was missing a few watts, but at least it was back. "It's about Rex, Tish. He was the first – and last – man I ever slept with. We started goin' out together in high school, but then Rex went away to St. John's to do auto mechanics, and later I decided to go away to school too. But I didn't really want to, all I wanted was to get married and have youngsters with Rex." A lone tear trickled down Osmond's cheek and her lips started to quiver.

Delmont said, quickly, "So, what happened to your relationship with Rex?"

"Well, he got in with a hard crowd in town, started drinkin' too much, takin' drugs - acid, mushrooms, cocaine. You know what mushrooms are, Tish?"

"Yes, Sally. Magic mushrooms – hallucinogenic fungi whose main ingredient is psilocybin. They work something like LSD. Some mental health experts believe they have a therapeutic role to play in treating mental disorders, but we aren't allowed to carry out research on them because they are illegal."

"That's right, magic mushrooms. Easy to find around these parts. All over the cow pastures.

"Anyway, Rex and I both came back to Setback, but he was changed. He used to be really laid back and funny, and you could always count on him – I'd have trusted him with my life before the drugs. He kept on doin' the drugs and goin' on the booze all the time when we got back, and I was about to break up with him when I found out I was pregnant with Bette. I was so excited to be havin' a child, and Rex was too when I told him. But I said, "Rex, you can't be no part of this child's life, or my life if you don't get off them drugs and cut down on the alcohol." And he did, straight away. He was just like his old self again, and we were so happy. And when Bette was born, well, you'd never want a better man or father than Rex, he even got a job fixin' cars – I was livin' with my parents, not workin' – and every minute he wasn't at work, he was home, feedin' the baby, bathin' her, changin' her, waitin' hand and foot on me. He'd moved into my parents' place, and we were talkin' about gettin' married that summer, but then . . .."

"What happened?" Delmont got the words out just in time, she figured. She could tell Sally was about to go off like a whistling kettle again.

"He went right back to his old habits when Bette was about six months old. I told him to knock it off, and he quit doin' drugs and drinkin' and stayin' out all hours of the night for a week or two. Then he went back on it all with a vengeance. So, I kicked him out – he went back to his mother's house. His father died in a car accident when he was five, and sometimes I wonder if that wasn't what was wrong with him. He never spoke about it, see – not to me or his mother or anyone. And she remarried, and her new man didn't take to the kids. Not that he beat them or anythin,' he just didn't want them around."

Anyway, I ran into his mother a few weeks later, and she told me Rex wouldn't leave the house anymore, and that he'd stopped talkin' to her and her husband and everyone else. I had half a mind to go over to see him, but I never. And then, he did it."

Sally stopped talking. She had turned white as a snow goose. Tish got up, opened the bottle of wine Sally had brought, half-filled a small wine glass and placed it in front of her. The girl took three long swallows. Some colour returned to her face.

"Sally, you don't have to talk about this any longer if it's too upsetting."

"No, that's okay. Might as well finish the story. His mother never heard a sound out of him for two whole days and nights, and when she went to check on him the third day, the bedroom door was locked and there was not a sound comin' from inside. When her husband got home from fishin', he pried the door open and found Rex hangin' from the rafters. He'd took a couple of tiles out of the ceilin' to get the rope around them."

Osmond's face crumpled and down she went, into another spasm of uncontrollable misery. Jesus Christ thought Delmont, I am surrounded. She went to the bathroom and came back with a roll of toilet paper, which she placed on the table.

The girl finally stopped crying and blew her nose. She looked miserably at Delmont and whispered, "I'm sorry. It's just that I loved him so much, and I feel so guilty. And poor Bette, growin' up without a father."

"It's best to get it all out, girl. Don't mind doing it in front of me: that's what friends are for. As a professional, though, I want to tell you that whatever happened to Rex, it wasn't your fault, there was nothing you could do to save him. He needed someone like me, and even then, there are no guarantees. Suicide is complicated, and it sounds as though Rex had a lot of trauma from his childhood and no way to deal with it. Guilt always goes with death, Sally. They're best friends."

"Thanks, Tish. I'm goin' to take off now before I flood your kitchen."

"Okay, see you Monday, then. I'm going to hole up here for the weekend and relax. You take care of yourself, Ms. Osmond. And as for Bette growing up without a father, my parents divorced when I was two years old, and I've rarely seen my father since. But I've got a wonderful mother. I don't feel any loss on that score. Bette has a wonderful mother too – no, don't start up again."

Osmond smiled through the tears in her eyes.

When the girl had gone, Delmont got ready to go for a run. With any luck, she wouldn't hear the sound of a human voice - crying or pleading or mourning - for two whole days. Sally was young, healthy, and undamaged for the most part, as far as Delmont could tell. Her main problem would be to find some man who wasn't a drug addict or alcoholic. A significant problem in a place like Setback, it seemed. Too bad she couldn't take Sally back to Chicago with her. But that would cause problems for Delmont herself.

Chapter 4

On Monday morning, Sally came into Tish's office almost as soon as she had taken off her coat.

"Did you get all the stuff put away, after, Tish?"

"Yes, I did. Although I need to move the furniture out of the lavender room before I can turn it into a fitness room. I'll need some help with that. Do you know anyone I can hire?"

"I can get my brother Rick to help you. He's a bit of a handyman and strong as a bull."

"That would be great. What does he charge?"

Sally laughed. "Charge? He won't charge you nothin'. Around here, everyone helps each other. If you offered him money, it would be an insult."

"Well, that's a fine tradition, indeed."

"Beer, he drinks beer, not the hard stuff. His brand is Black Horse, you can get it at any of the convenience stores. It's brewed in St. John's. I'll call him and see when he's free. When's good for you?"

"Any time after work. Just let me know when he's coming and I'm not buying beer for anyone, I'll pay them, and they can do whatever with it. Sally, alcohol is a big issue in this town and surrounding towns. Not adding to the issue, I was brought here to try and get it under control. Sorry."

"No worries, they'll do it, beer or no beer. I'll go back to my office and call him."

Five minutes later, there was a knock on Tish's door.

"Come in. Oh, it's you, Sally. You don't have to knock unless I'm with a client."

"Okay. I just talked to Rick, him and his buddy Dave Langdon can go to your place this evenin' around five. Is that all right?"

"Sounds great; I'll leave work early."

Sally went out of the office and then came back in. "Tish, I got to tell you somethin'."

"What is it? You look pretty serious." Sally did look serious. And her cheeks were pink. What fresh hell was this?

"It's Rick, Tish. He's a male whore. He'd screw anythin' with two feet and a heartbeat."

Delmont looked nonplussed. She *felt* nonplussed. Was Sally trying to tell her that her brother was a sexual predator? Why in the hell would she send a sexual predator to her house? Maybe they were as common as drunks and drug addicts in Setback. Oh, fuck.

"What?"

"Rick, he's a ladies' man. He likes women, especially good-lookin' ones like you."

"Well, you just tell your brother I'm a lesbian, Sally. That should give him pause."

Sally's face turned red. "Oh, Tish, I never thought . . . I didn't know. I'll tell him, I will."

"I'm joking, Sally. I'll handle him. He's not . . . I mean, he doesn't have a record for sexual assault or anything, does he?"

Sally looked horrified. "Oh, Jesus no, Tish. He's harmless, just a big flirt. I'll tell him to keep it down, will I?"

"I'll tell him myself, Sally." And she would.

When Delmont got home after work, two well-built young men on three-wheel all-terrain vehicles were parked next to her deck. Each of them had a bottle of beer in one hand and a cigarette in the other hand. Great, more alcoholics. And driving under the influence, no less.

She stepped out of her rented car, walked over and extended her hand. "I'm Tish, thanks for coming over to help me out." She forced a stiff smile.

The dark-haired one who looked like Sally said, "I'm Rick. Welcome to Setback, sweetheart. Movin' furniture is no big deal. We're not at nothin' these days anyway, what with no fishery and no fish plant. We got lots of time on our hands."

"I didn't think you were allowed to drive those things on main roads," Delmont said, nodding at the three-wheelers.

Rick grinned. "Not strictly, no. But this is a small place,

and no one says nothin' unless you runs a youngster over, and no one has done that yet."

"Yeah, I guess you're probably all related here, aren't you?" Which would explain a lot. But not the absence of extra fingers and toes.

"If not, we've been neighbours for centuries. You want to go for a ride or what, darlin'?"

"Um, thanks but no. Not my kind of vehicle. Also, I suspect they do a lot of damage to the environment. And it would be better for your mental and physical health to walk in the woods rather than use those things. My professional opinion, of course. Personally, I don't care what you do."

Damn, that was too harsh. She'd probably have to get someone else to move her stuff. Someone older, maybe, who didn't patronize her with "sweetheart" and "darling." They couldn't help it, she knew – you couldn't expect rednecks anywhere to pick up on misogyny.

The men looked at each other, and then at Tish. Rick said, "You're a hard case, Tish. Lucky you're good lookin', or you wouldn't get away with it. Good lookin' and a friend of Sally's."

"Oh, I'm not all that bad," Tish shot back. "You'll get used to me." But will I ever get used to you? Or this place?

Behind her back, as she led them into the house, Tish knew they were sizing her up - and probably making rude gestures. She gritted her teeth and reminded herself that one of them was Sally's brother and that they wouldn't be around for long.

At the door, the two men started to remove their green rubber boots.

"You can leave them on."

Rick said, "It's bad luck to enter a house with rubber boots on in Newfoundland."

Tish laughed. "Really. I guess that comes from having a broom taken to you by an irate housewife if there was mud on those boots."

The two men laughed and agreed that it probably did.

It took them fifteen minutes to sort out the moving, and afterwards, Delmont offered them a cup of the coffee she had been making while they worked. "Also, there's tea there if you'd rather it."

"You don't have either beer around, do you?" Dave said. Rick looked as though he was still sulking from what she'd said earlier.

"No, I don't. Drinking and alcoholism is rampant in this town and area and I'm not assisting anyone in it. I'll pay for your services. I have non-alcoholic beer if you would like that." Both looked at each other. Rick spoke. "Belly-wash, non-alcoholic beer is like a vibrator with no batteries."

"Excuse me?"

"Sweetheart, non-alcoholic beer will fill you up. But like a vibrator with no batteries, you won't get much of a buzz off it."

Delmont ignored the comment and changed the subject. The three sat at the kitchen table, drinking tea and coffee.

"What do I owe you? I like to keep things fair and square."

"Jesus, no, duckie, we does stuff like this all the time for nothin'."

"As I said, it's only fair. I might need you again sometime, you never know."

Delmont fervently hoped this would not be the case, but it probably would be. If she needed a couple of people to do some heavy lifting, she would likely have to put up with Rick, or risk offending Sally. She suddenly wished she'd turned down the contract, although she knew the experience would be useful down the road.

"Listen, honey," said Rick, "any time ya needs a hand or a lift with anythin', call me - here write down me number.

 Do you mind if I have a smoke?" As he asked, Rick pulled a green and white cigarette pack out of the pocket of his plaid shirt.

"Yeah, I do, actually. Especially since it's not my house."

"Not a problem, we'll go out on the deck and have a smoke." The two men put on their rubber boots and headed outside. While they smoked, Delmont made a few work-related notes on a yellow pad she kept on the table. Occasionally, she glanced out the window at Rick and Dave. Rick was certainly handsome. Of course, he would be, being Sally's brother. Dave was not bad looking either. You could tell they were labourers by their physiques. Too bad about the rest, but one of them might be good for a quick roll in the hay – although she would have to be careful on that score. Business and pleasure didn't mix. She would be stuck here for months without a break, however. Oh, Lord. She quickly derailed that train of thought.

"So, can we have another tea, Tish, or have ya got somethin' to do?"

"I've got some work to go over. But I'll have one more coffee and then as I said I have work to go over."

They stayed for an hour, drinking tea, and smoking on the deck. She had difficulty understanding some of what they said because of their accents and rapid rate of speech. There was a heap of local gossip, which she'd mentally recorded – some of it, anyway - and would jot down later. The one thing she understood perfectly was that Setback had a police officer – RCMP – that must refer to the famous Mounties – named Cocksucker Ross. At least that was how the two men referred to him. Apparently, he was new in town and hounded people on ATVs. Also, he was known to stop every car on the weekends to check for drunk drivers. Well, thank God someone was concerned about drinking and driving – the locals didn't seem to give it a second thought. She was looking forward to meeting the RCMP officers and discussing the town's problems with another set of professionals.

When it was time for Rick and Dave to leave, Delmont asked them if they were sure they were okay to drive.

Rick said, "Sweetheart, we only had five beers each. I often drives with two dozen in me."

Delmont was floored. Sally hadn't mentioned that her brother was a raging alcoholic and a dangerous one. She didn't know what to say to him. What she wanted to say to him – "Rick, you're an asshole" – wouldn't be helpful.

Rick took her silence for interest. "I starts drinkin' before dinner and drives home from the nightclub around midnight and never puts a scratch on the bike."

"That's a lot of drinking. And driving. Aren't you afraid your luck will run out? I mean, the odds are that down the road you'll hit someone or destroy your liver. Or both."

The two men laughed. "Jesus, no, b'y, we does that all the time. It's only beer, like water when ya get used to it."

When Delmont pulled out of her driveway the following day, she noticed the tire tracks from the ATVs. Rick and Dave had sent rocks and earth flying when they left the night before. She thought Setback was like some parts of Chicago. Not parts she had spent any time in, or ever would.

Chapter 5

THE NEXT MORNING DELMONT THANKED SALLY FOR SENDING her brother and his friend to help her.

"Rick's good like that."

Delmont closed the office door. This wasn't going to be easy. "Sally, I don't know how to broach this, but your brother – does he have an alcohol problem? He told me how much he drinks, and it's far more than is good for him."

Osmond giggled. "Oh, Tish, Rick, he lives every day like it's his last. Not a chick nor child to worry about. And he goes through women like toothpaste. They all drink like that around here. It doesn't hurt them none. It's only beer, mostly."

"Sally, if he keeps it up, he'll destroy his physical and mental health. You know that."

"Oh, don't worry. Someday some woman will put the

clamps on him and then he'll only be livin' it up on the weekends."

Delmont wanted to ask her if the women minded being prison wardens to men who never grew up, but she bit her tongue.

At lunchtime on Friday, Delmont and Osmond walked around the little town, which sat at the base of an inlet three kilometres long. The wind was excruciatingly cold. The two women were muffled up from head to toe. Whitecaps swayed on the water in the harbour like gulls.

"You're goin' to have to go to the post office and get a box, Tish. We don't get mail delivered."

"I don't really need one, Sally. I get my mail at the office. Sally, what is the RCMP's role here? Don't you have any local police?"

"Yes and no, St. John's, Corner Brook on the west coast of the island and Labrador City in Labrador are the only places with a police force. The Royal Newfoundland Constabulary, actually the oldest police force in Canada, datin' back to 1841. They're the only police force in Canada not armed. Everywhere else we have Mounties. But they're okay, most of them. They don't come from here, generally, they come from the mainland. Not to say that some Newfoundlanders aren't RCMP cops, but if they are, they get sent somewhere else in Canada, usually. Keeps them from bein' too thick with the people they look after, I suppose. They're pretty easy on the eyes, most of them. You'll see."

Delmont smiled. Perhaps Sally could snag one for herself, a nice tall man in a red uniform. Because there didn't seem to be much on offer in the way of decent men in Setback.

Later in the afternoon, Sally asked Delmont if she would be available for a meet-and-greet the following Friday, at noon, with the mayor, council, fire chief, and some volunteer fire department members, along with the three members of the RCMP stationed in Setback, and some business people. It would be held in the town office, and the town would supply lunch.

"Sure, Sally. Bill Welsh will be here then, and he'll come. By the way, would you like to come over tomorrow to help me paint the lavender room? The vibe is much too peaceful for a workout room - I bought some red paint."

"Sure, if I can get someone to watch Bette."

"Okay."

"Tish, I'm leavin' early today. Would you mind lockin' up, and settin' the alarm? There's a safe in the buildin', so we got to have an alarm system."

"Sure thing, Sally."

Sally arrived at Delmont's place the next morning, the psychologist was wearing an old pair of jeans and an oversize T-shirt. A bright red band covered the front of her hair. There was a fire in the fireplace, crackling and spitting as though it was desperate to leave the confines of the hearth.

"I see the smoke comin' out of the chimney when I pulled in – where did you get the firewood, Tish?"

"Oh, it was in the old barn."

"I never thought a city girl like you would know how to light a fire."

"We had a fireplace at home when I was growing up. My mother and I used to use it a lot in the winter. Just for the ambience. It was one of those suburban things, didn't throw off a lot of heat."

"I love fireplaces. Me and Rex were goin' to have one in our house."

Was Sally going to start crying again? If so, Delmont would have to ease herself back a bit from the relationship. She got enough emotional upheaval at work; she needed peace outside of it. But Sally only looked a bit wistful, not tragic.

"Yes, I do too. I've been using this one all week, it's been so cold. Plus, it's just so damn peaceful in front of it, with a good book. Or even with work. I expect it triggers ancestral memories at some deep level. A cave, a fire – now all we need is a caveman or two."

Sally laughed. "That would be nice."

Tish smiled. "You never know what might happen in front of that fireplace. It has potential."

The morning passed quickly. Delmont was glad of Sally's help; she knew what she was doing when it came to painting. The room was small, and they had the walls and ceiling primed by late afternoon.

"Let's go down and have some coffee before you go, Sally. Or would you like a glass of wine? I have red and white."

"I'd love a glass, don't care what kind. I go back and forth."

Delmont got herself a mug of coffee and a goblet of red wine for Sally. The girl looked particularly fetching at the moment, with a streak of white paint splashed across her nose. She reminded Delmont of a black cat she'd had as a child, who had a similar streak across his nose. For a moment she was acutely homesick for Chicago. She gave herself an invisible shake.

"Sally, I'm going to need a cleaning woman once every two weeks or so - do you know anyone?"

Sally looked nonplussed. "A cleanin' woman, haven't you ever done housework before?"

Tish grinned. "Yes, but I don't make a habit of it. If they'd put me up in an apartment, I'd have coped, but this place is big, and I don't want to spend my free time as a charwoman. So, do you know anyone? It doesn't matter about the cost, my employer will foot the bill."

"I can probably get one of my mother's cousin's daughters to do it. They wouldn't mind a bit of spare money, and they're all good at cleanin'. But, Tish, how will you ever get a man if you can't clean house?"

Delmont bit back her snort. She had been in Setback long enough to note that the locals were very house-proud. It was almost a religion, having a clean house.

"There are other ways to a man's heart, Sally. And speaking of men, have you seen any possibilities around here?"

Now the girl did look tragic, but not tearful, thank all the gods.

"I never looked at no one since Rex passed. Can't imagine sleepin' with another man. He was the only one I ever did sleep with, and I loved him so much."

"I know, Sally. And grief can't be rushed. It has to run its course. I was just wondering if anyone had caught your eye even for a moment. If there was anyone you thought was attractive, even if you didn't want to get involved with him."

Now Sally's expression was a mix of shame and - could it be delight?

"Spill the beans, Sally."

"Oh, Tish, you got to keep this quiet. I do kind of like someone, not the way I felt for Rex, but there's this new Mountie . . .."

Delmont suppressed her smile. Well, so there was a Mountie for Sally after all. Good for her. She only hoped that the Mountie had noticed Sally as well. It would be hard not to notice her, though – she was so much finer looking than most of the local women.

"His name is Terry Ross, and he's from Saskatchewan. Twenty-three and as tall as a tree, and handsome as – I don't know. He's just handsome. And he's got this quiet way about him, this thing he gives off – like his strength isn't just in his body but in his mind too. Like he's intelligent and responsible and . . . oh, I don't know. He's come in my office a few times, and I got the feelin' he likes me, but I'm probably just a desperate woman, and . . .."

"Terry Ross. Yes, your brother and his friend were talking about him the other night. Only they called him Cocksucker Ross."

"Oh, Tish, they're a couple of dickheads, even if one of them is my brother. Terry is only doin' his job. We would be in a sad state with no Mounties to protect us. "

"So, you like him, do you?"

"I don't know. I want to flirt with him, but part of me won't allow it to happen."

"You don't have to rush things. If he just got here, you have plenty of time. But he sounds like the kind of man you and Bette could build a good life with. Hey – I take that back – who knows what he is? But if your intuition is telling you he's the type of man you need, I would listen to it. Sally, I know you loved Rex, but he was a drug addict and most likely an alcoholic. And from what I've seen, there's a lot of that in Setback. Someone from outside, someone who isn't damaged might be just what the angels have in mind for you. And Rex would want that for you because I know he loved you and Bette even if he couldn't be a husband and father."

And now the tears came. Delmont sighed and got up from the table and went in search of the Kleenex box. She'd have to buy another one, and make sure it stayed in the kitchen.

When she returned, Sally was no longer leaking.

"I know I got to move on, Tish, but it's harder to do than say. You'll meet Terry on Friday at the meet-and-greet."

"Can't wait. You're not afraid I'll sweep him up, are you? No, I'm just kidding."

"He's single and fair game. I bet when you sees him, you'll say he's somethin' else."

Delmont thought he probably was something else, something far better than Sally was ever going to find in Setback. "I'm sure he's lovely, but I'm not in the market for a man right now. Besides, I can't ride a horse?"

"Ride a horse? What do you mean?"

"Well, in the movies, the Mounties are always on horses. Don't they ride to music or something? Some kind of dressage thing?"

"I'll have to ask him if he has a horse back home on the Prairies. Tish, can I ask *you* somethin'?"

"Sure. I might not answer, but you can ask."

"Don't you want kids?"

"Not really, although if I ever settle down, I might have one or two. Depends on the guy, I suppose. He'll have to make good money because the cost of childcare is crazy where I come from. The grandmothers of Chicago have their own lives, I'm afraid. But I could have a live-in nanny, I guess. Should have married that lawyer. Although he would have taken me to the cleaners if we ever got divorced."

Sally looked as though she were listening to Delmont speak a foreign language. And in a way, Delmont thought, she was.

"My life is Bette. I can't imagine not havin' her. She got me through Rex's death."

"That's wonderful. Don't you have to get home now? I thought your mother wanted to go out and you've got to look after Bette."

"Oh, Jesus, is that the time? I do have to go. Thanks for listenin', Tish. You're goin' to have to start chargin' me soon."

"That's okay – thanks for the help with the painting. We should get it all done by next weekend if you can come back and give me a hand."

At the door, Delmont kissed Sally gently on the cheek. She smelled of paint and wine and whatever she had washed her hair with that morning. The girl hugged her and went out into a cold wind that cut Delmont like a knife before she managed to shut the door.

Chapter 6

"TISH, YOU'LL NEED A MAN TO KEEP YOU COMPANY, TO KEEP you safe in that drafty old house the winter."

Delmont rolled her eyes. "I admit it was rather windy on Saturday. The house cracked and squeaked all night. But I'm used to wind – they call Chicago the Windy City, you know. It's just as cold in the winter as it is here, but not as – well, dismal."

"No, I never knew that Tish. So, you don't mind bein' alone over there?"

"Not unless you think I'm in any danger."

"Oh, no, my dear – nothin's goin' to happen to you in Setback." Sally seemed shocked at the suggestion. "But wouldn't you like a warm body next to you in bed?" Her grin was impish.

"Yeah, I would. And that body even has a name. Bella."

"Bella?" Sally looked uncertainly at Delmont.

"Actually, she's my dog, a light brown miniature dachshund, I had to leave her with my sister Jen, and I sure do miss her. My sister Jen owns her sister Lady. Bella is overweight and slow. Lady is slim and hyper. We rescued them from a shelter. We love them so much. Dachshunds have a unique personality."

"That's one thing I miss since becomin' single, Tish, a warm body."

"Don't worry, Sally – there's always your Mountie."

A flush bloomed under Sally's dusky skin.

"And there must be other guys in Setback that aren't a complete waste of time."

"Oh yes, there's a few eligible bachelors around."

"Really?" Delmont found this hard to believe, but she was willing to keep an open mind.

"Well, one of the fire captains is hot. Jimmy Parsons, but for some reason, he can't keep a steady. He dates a woman for a few months and then moves on. A bit of a gigolo if you ask me. Drives a red Corvette in summer, beautiful car. And then there's Rock McGee, a bouncer at the Longview nightclub. Twice divorced, leaves the club every Friday and Saturday night with a different woman. God knows what he's got. You'll meet Jimmy at the social on Friday."

"I can't wait, I have a soft spot for older men who drive red cars," said Delmont. Christ Almighty, the girl needed to be airlifted out of this godawful place and spend at least a year in therapy. Perhaps then she'd know what an eligible man looked like. Pity stabbed the psychologist's heart like a dart of raw wind off the North Atlantic.

"Why are we single at our ages?"

"I don't know, Sally. Just lucky, I guess."

Bill Grant arrived on time for his appointment. When he walked in, he tried to put his arms around Delmont.

"I'm sorry, Mr. Grant, but that's not appropriate behaviour. Sit down and tell me how you're feeling. Did you get the prescription for antidepressants from your GP, and are you taking them?" Delmont summoned up what she hoped would pass for a friendly smile to take the sting out of her rejection of his hug. He looked like she'd just peed in his cornflakes, as the saying went, but he'd get over it, as she knew from long experience.

"I never meant nothin' by it, Doctor. Yes, I saw Dr. Quigley and got the drugs."

"So, have you taken the medication as prescribed?"

"I have."

"Do you find any change in your mood?"

"I do. My beer consumption has gone from a dozen or a dozen and a half a day to less than a six-pack. And I can say, I feel a little better. My thoughts are not as negative."

"Well, that's an improvement," said Tish. Not much of

one, he'd probably die of cirrhosis before he got around to killing himself. "But you need to cut down much further than that. I can't stress enough how inimical alcohol is to good mental health."

Grant acted as if he hadn't heard what she'd said. "And you know what, doc? I'm feelin' a lot better. I don't have that bastard Jack on my mind as near as much as I used to. And the wife is not naggin' me as much. Ya know, we weren't gettin' along before Jack passed. Any day at all, I expects to come home and find her and the cat gone. She has a big white tomcat named Finbar, and she likes the cat more than she likes me."

Delmont smiled inwardly. Of course, she liked the cat better than she liked her husband. For one thing, the cat was probably sober more often.

"Why do you call your deceased best friend a bastard, Mr. Grant?"

"Well, Doc, for what he did. It's all right for him, he's at peace or at rest or whatever. It's the people he left behind who will never get over what he did. When I gets up in heaven, the first thing I'm goin' to do to Jack when I see him is give him a punch in the mouth."

"I'm not sure people punch other people in the mouth in heaven, but you never know. Anger at the dead is a perfectly normal feeling to have, Mr. Grant. Anger and guilt often go hand in hand with death. Does this anger make you feel uncomfortable, or is it a positive emotion, do you think?"

"I guess it's a good thing. Anyway, sweetheart, that's one fuckin' thing that's not comin' out of my head. I can't wait to give him a smack in the mouth, he's fucked me up majorly, and his family is sufferin' as well."

"And what are you doing to fill up your days now that you are no longer drinking so much?" Only about as much as a regular alcoholic anywhere else. If there were an Alcoholic Olympics, any one of the male residents of Setback would be a contender.

"Well, I'm in the woods on any day the weather's good. Cuttin' logs and firewood, snarin' a scattered rabbit. An occasional boil-up at the cabin. It passes the time and keeps my head sane. Not to change the topic, Doc, but I hear you're livin' in the Squires' house out on the Point Road?"

"Yes."

"That's a nice spot out there. The Squires used to buy firewood from me."

"I'm really enjoying that fireplace, Mr. Grant. I'm going to need some more wood soon. There was some left in the old barn, but not enough for the winter, which I'm told can last until June in these parts."

"I sells firewood."

"Well, I need to buy some. How much do you charge?"

"Fifty bucks a load, sixty junked up."

"Junked up?"

"Cut in junks ready for the stove or fireplace."

"Oh, cut in *chunks*. Or cut to length, as we say in the States. I need to buy two loads."

"Not a problem. I'll deliver it sometime on Saturday, most likely in the mornin'."

"Fine. I might be out, but you can put it in the barn and give Sally an invoice for it next week."

Grant looked sulky. "Invoice? I don't do invoices. Cash only."

"All right, Mr. Grant. Cash it is." So, he didn't want to pay taxes. She wondered where he thought the money came from for the free healthcare Canadians enjoyed, or money for the roads and so many other things. He didn't think about that, obviously. Or much else. Anyway, she didn't mind taking the money out of her own pocket for the pleasure of having a fire in the grate on all those cold winter nights to come. Better a fire than one of these men.

As they walked to the door, Grant said, "See you Saturday, sweetheart, most likely in the mornin'." He turned around and she thought he was going to try to touch her, so she shut the door. She would cancel his sessions soon and leave him to Shandal. The antidepressants were working, thank God, and he wasn't a good candidate for therapy, at least not therapy with her. Shandal was a better fit.

On Friday, Sally buzzed Delmont a little after twelve to tell her the meet and greet was in progress.

When the psychologist walked into the meeting room, everyone in attendance stared at her. They were all men. So, no women held positions of responsibility in this community. Well, that was hardly surprising.

Sally came forward and took her to a short, fat man whom she introduced as Mayor White. He had a pleasant face and a firm, dry grip.

"Welcome to our town, Dr. Delmont. If there's anything I can do to assist you or make your job more manageable, I'm only a phone call away."

"Why thank you, Mr. White. There is one thing – ever since I arrived here, I've been wondering where the name Setback came from. No one seems to know."

"Well, Doctor -"

"Tish."

"Tish – and I'm Mike – we don't really know where the name came from. There's no record of its origin that I know of, but the story is, is that it's called Setback because it's set back from the sea. You know, we're at the end of an inlet. What we do know is that it was settled in 1621, the same year as Ferryland on the Southern Shore on the Avalon, which was settled by Lord Baltimore. Both communities are the second oldest in Newfoundland after Cupids in Conception Bay, which was settled in 1610."

"Ferryland? What a lovely name. Newfoundland has so many interesting placenames."

"We're an old colony, and many European nations came here to fish. They left some of their languages in the names. Ferryland comes from the Portuguese for a small promontory, although its current population is mostly Irish. Most Irish in the world, I'm told. I'm from there myself, originally. I don't know if you've met Corporal Campbell yet, first placement was in Ferryland in the early eighties. He speaks highly of the people on the Southern Shore."

"As you probably know, Mr. White, there's a large Irish population where I'm from, Chicago – St. Patrick's Day is a big deal there."

"Well, the fella that founded Ferryland, that Baltimore fella, couldn't take the cold, so he went south and founded what would become Baltimore in Maryland."

"And how did Black Tree come by its name; do you know?"

"Sure, it's the only community on the island with thousands of black spruce in it. Black spruce grows right across Canada, the northern part of it, anyway It's a tough tree, just like those of us who live here with it."

"Now, Mr. White, I'm takin' Tish away from you. She needs to circulate." Sally took Tish's arm, and she was introduced to the town councillors in attendance; all were male except one. Next came Sergeant Jack Campbell, who was in charge of the local RCMP detachment. He told Delmont to call him if there was any trouble, he could help her with.

"I saved the best for last, Tish," Sally whispered. They were approaching a very tall young man in uniform.

"Tish, this is Constable Terry Ross."

Delmont had to agree that he was a prize specimen of

manhood, and when he turned a twenty-four-carat smile on her, she felt it right down to her knees.

"Dr. Delmont, hello. Sally has mentioned you once or a hundred times."

"Tish, please. Sally is my right hand here. Couldn't function without her." And someday, young man, I hope you feel the same way about her.

"Where are you staying, if you don't mind me asking?"

"South Side Point Road, in a green two-story house, the last one out on the point."

"I've seen that house – lovely old place. I patrol out there late at night sometimes."

"Good to know that the Mounties are keeping an eye on me – you're famous for always getting your man, aren't you? The bad guy, I mean."

"Oh, yes, Dr. – Tish – we always get our man." And then, with a sidelong glance at Sally, he said, "Not always our woman, though."

Delmont was glad to see that look. Apparently, Sally had seen it too, because her eyes were shining and there was a red spot on each cheek.

Within an hour, Delmont had met and spoken to everyone in attendance. Working with these people would be enjoyable, they meant well and had a kind of innocence she rarely encountered in Chicago, or anywhere else she'd been.

———————————

Chapter 7

———————————

EARLY THE NEXT MORNING — TOO EARLY — DELMONT HEARD A vehicle enter her yard. She got up and threw on a pair of jeans and a T-shirt, hauled on her coat and boots, and made her way outdoors. Bill Grant was throwing what he called "junks" of firewood from his pickup towards the barn door.

"You're earlier than I expected."

"I wanted to get the wood delivered and stored before noon. Saturday's a drinkin' day in Setback."

Delmont shook her head. Every day was a "drinking day" in Setback. No wonder the island had the highest rate in Canada of so many diseases. Between the alcohol abuse and the local diet, it was a good thing most of its inhabitants were loaded up with tough peasant genes.

"Is that so? Perhaps it shouldn't be for you, Mr. Grant.

Come to the door when you're finished, and I'll give you your money."

Three hours later, there was a knock on the door.

"I stored the two loads of wood."

"I didn't expect you to stack it for me, Mr. Grant. But thank you. Would you like a cup of coffee. Or tea?" No one in Chicago drank tea. She didn't think you could get it even in a hotel restaurant. But next to beer, tea was the favourite drink in Setback. Sally had taught her how to make a decent cup in case she ever had to.

Grant's face lit up. "Sure, I'd love a cup of tea. Don't suppose you got a beer?"

"No, Mr. Grant, I do not."

"Call me Bill – and you're Tish, aren't you?"

Why, why, why had she asked him in? Too late now. "No, Mr. Grant. You're Mr. Grant and I'm Dr. Delmont. It's a Doctor-patient relationship, not a friendship."

Grant didn't say anything for a moment. "Well, honey – Dr. Honey - anytime you buys wood from me, remember, I'll stack it free of charge."

Delmont didn't reply; she went to her purse, extracted two fifty-dollar bills, and passed them to him.

"You don't have to give me that much. Eighty would be fine."

"No, you put the wood away for me. Next time, I'll do that myself. I like the exercise."

He looked her over from head to foot, slowly, so she'd

know he was doing it. What an asshole. "Sure, keeps you in shape, all that runnin' you do. I sees you sometimes, out on the road, goin' like a deer. I'll just go out on the deck and take my coveralls off and be right back in."

"What do you want in your tea?"

"A drop of milk and three spoonfuls of sugar."

"Will skim milk do?"

"Christ, woman, you only got cow's milk, do you?"

"Were you looking for goat's milk?" Sally hadn't mentioned that.

"No, I wants Carnation milk in me tea, same as everyone."

"I don't know what that is – You can have it with skim milk, or you can have it black."

She made the tea, got herself a coffee and sat down. How long was he going to hang around? Well, that was up to her, really. She had a feeling he wasn't going to go soon or quietly.

"Beautiful spot you have here."

"Yes. Great old house. Sally Osmond helped me move in."

"Sweet girl that Sally," Bill said. "Her brother Rick is a prick."

Well, I think you two might have something in common, Delmont didn't say.

He saw her look. "It's a long story sweetheart. We don't like each other."

Delmont ignored the comment. She made small talk about the weather, the community, and the state of the roads. She was bored to death and really wanted to get at her computer.

There was a lot of work to be done, plus she needed to write to her family and her colleagues.

"Where's the washroom?"

"Upstairs, right at the end of the hall."

A couple of minutes later, she heard him call out. She went to the bottom of the stairs

"Yes, Mr. Grant, what is it?"

"I'm in a bit of a pickle up here, Doc. Was wonderin' if you could help me out."

What in the hell kind of trouble could he have possibly gotten in upstairs? Had he jammed his hand in the window? But why would he have even opened it? She made an irritated sound and ascended the stairs.

Grant was standing outside the bathroom door, stark naked, an erection pointed proudly at her. At least that's what it seemed by the look on his face.

She felt a tingle of fear and a desire to burst out laughing.

"Mr. Grant, get your clothes on and get out of my house before I call the police."

Grant's face quickly moved from shock to belligerence. "I comes here, stacks all that wood, has a nice, friendly cup of tea with you, and just because I thinks maybe you'd like a bit more than some wood, you're goin' to get the cops on me? Who do you think you are, anyway, sweetheart?"

"I think I'm your psychologist, Mr. Grant, not your 'sweetheart.' And perhaps it's customary in Setback for a woman to have sex with a man just because he drops off a load of wood and stacks it, but I can assure you it's not part of my culture. In Chicago, I would call the police if a man made unwanted sexual advances. And that's what I'm going to do here as well if you don't get dressed and get out right now. And from now on, you'll see Dr. Shandal."

"You fuckin' bitch, I'll be glad to go to Dr. Shandal, even if he is a foreigner. He's a man, and he's a real Doctor." Grant turned around, walked into the bathroom and slammed the door.

Delmont went to her bedroom and closed the door. She waited until she heard his truck peal out of the yard, and then went downstairs, poured herself a mug of coffee and put a hefty shot of Rémy Martin in it. Her hands were shaking and didn't stop until she'd swallowed half the mug's contents and taken several deep breaths. And then the door opened. Oh, damn and hell, what now?

"Tish, hi, it's only me, Sally. What are you up to?"

Delmont composed her face into a welcoming mask. "Sally, how are you? I was just going up to do some work, but that can wait. Sit down and have a coffee with me." And please don't start crying or I'm going to pour the rest of this over your head.

"I saw Bill Grant drive out of here – he drop off the wood, or what?"

Delmont burst out laughing, a high-pitched, slightly hysterical laugh that made Sally look at her in surprise. But she wasn't going to explain, oh no.

"Yes, Sally, he's very friendly. What are you up to today?"

"Well, I was wonderin' if you wanted to go for a walk or anythin' – or I could help you with some housework if you need me to."

"Why thanks, Sally, but I'm going for a run later – I really need something more challenging than a walk today – and I have to get some work done before that. As for housework, no, that girl you recommended came a few days ago and did a great job on the place."

"Well, I guess I'd better be goin' then." Sally's face suddenly brightened. "Terry Ross called me last night. He said he'd take me and Bette for a drive tomorrow if I wanted."

Delmont smiled. A man who knew how to court a woman, that Terry Ross. Not someone who was just going to show up with a load of wood and an erection. "What did you tell him, Sally girl?"

"I told him I'd love to. Do you think I should've?"

"Of course – don't you? He's a beauty."

"That's right, you met him yesterday."

"I did, and I think you should jump his bones."

"Tish!" Sally's face was a study in scarlet. "What about Rex?"

Tish leaned forward and took the tall, dark girl's hand. It was warm and comforting. "Do you know what I think, Sally? I believe you're using Rex as an excuse not to move on. I think you're afraid you're not good enough for Constable Ross, that he might not want you because you have a child. You're probably afraid you might not love Ross if you got to know him, or maybe you're afraid he'll want to move out of Setback eventually. Actually, it's probably a combination of these things and a whole bunch of others neither one of us is aware of, but why don't you stop thinking and start living? One day at a time. Just go for the drive and see how it feels. If it feels wrong, don't go again. It's really that simple."

Sally got up and stretched and shook herself. Delmont thought that the movements were designed for her psyche as well as her body. She was glad she had spoken to the girl about Terry Ross, and she thought it was likely Sally would go out with him tomorrow.

Suddenly, the girl sat back down, and she now had a serious look on her face. "Tish, I got to tell you somethin'. About the Grants."

"What about them, Sally?" Oh, dear - more local gossip. She really didn't have the time or the inclination, but she didn't want to hurt Sally's feelings.

"The Grants are a mean bunch, all three of them. Bill has two brothers, Walter, and Mick, both older than him. Walter killed a man, Gerry Lyver, about ten years ago, for sleepin' with his wife. He served ten years for it, did his time up in Dorchester Penitentiary in the Province of New Brunswick. Been out a few years now. They got violent tempers and are jealous of their women, and they're big-time womanizers. So, I wouldn't be too nice to him if I were you."

"Don't worry, Sally, I wasn't too nice." Christ in a basket, Chicago was looking good. "How did Grant kill the man?"

"They had words at Longview, the bar I was tellin' you about. They calls Longview the swamp, and if you ever goes in there you'll know why. Anyway, Walter found out about the affair and threw it up in Gerry's face. The story is Walter was loaded drunk and challenged Gerry to a fight outside. But Gerry refused to fight with him. The story goes Walter went out and hid in the back seat of Gerry's car and waited for him. When Gerry got in, Walter put a knife to his throat and forced him to drive out this road, the one you're on. He said in court he never planned on killin' him, but he did, he stabbed Gerry in the neck. And then he walked back to town and got some gasoline and rags out of his shed and took his own vehicle back here. He set Gerry's car on fire and ran it out over an embankment into a gulch."

"Is that where the white cross is?"

"Yes. It's a tradition in Newfoundland to place white wooden crosses where people have been killed in car accidents. The Trans-Canada Highway from St. John's to Port aux Basques on the west coast has dozens and dozens of them. They call that gulch Dead Man's Gulch now."

"How morbid. And it wasn't exactly a car accident, either."

"There's more to this story. I'll fill you in at the office Monday mornin'."

Sally glanced at her watch. "I just remembered, Rick said

he'd come and get me here at one, he dropped me off, my car is in the garage. It's makin' a funny noise. I hope he's not on the beer yet. Saturdays are his favourite drinkin' days."

It seemed to Delmont that every day was a favourite drinking day for Sally's brother. With any luck, Terry Ross would take Sally to civilization someday. Perhaps she'd have a word with him, speed up the process.

As Sally turned to go through the door, Delmont put her hand on her shoulder. She turned, and Delmont kissed her quickly on the lips.

"Tish . . ."

The girl looked puzzled but not offended. "Sorry, Sally. Chicago girlfriend custom. Have a good time with Mr. Handsome tomorrow, now."

After Sally left, Delmont locked the door, the first time she had ever done so.

Chapter 8

ON MONDAY MORNING, SALLY WENT TO DELMONT'S OFFICE as soon as she had taken off her coat.

"Tish, how was your weekend?"

"Good, thanks. I got loads of work done and I slept well too." Not really, every time she heard a vehicle drive by, she'd had to check to make sure the door was bolted. "And how was your weekend, Sally?" Delmont gave Osmond a stage wink.

Sally's dark cheeks flushed even darker. "Oh, you mean goin' drivin' with Terry Ross. It was all right, I suppose." Her face erupted into a huge grin.

"I see. Well, that's great. Listen – do you want to help me with some more painting? I really can't live with that blue in the upstairs hall."

"Sure. This Saturday?"

"Yup."

"Tish, I told Rick that you bought two loads of firewood from Bill, and he said he had a couple of dozen loads of dry firewood that he'd give you for a good price. Said he'd be cheaper than Bill."

"Sally, I have enough firewood for the next two years. It's not like I'm heating the house with it. Besides, I don't want to start a firewood war in Setback."

"You might. Every man in Setback cuts firewood, and they all drool over good-lookin' women, especially women like you. They talk about your American accent, you know."

I bet they do, thought Delmont. That and other things they don't mention in front of Sally. "Tell Rick thanks, but no thanks, will you? Not to change the topic, but did you know I can't get cable TV?"

"Why?"

"Apparently, South Side Point Road is too far out, and if they were to run it out to me, they would charge me extra, per pole length. I said forget it. I'm not one to spend much time in front of a TV set anyway."

"I'll tell Rick."

When Delmont arrived home from work, there was a red Dodge pickup backed up in front of her barn door. Her heart began to beat faster, and she put her key inside her fist before she got out of the car. Perhaps she should go into the house and lock the door behind her. She shook off the thought – she couldn't stay spooked because of one random asshole, even if his brother was a killer. She walked to the unknown pickup and saw Sally's brother tossing pieces of birch into the barn.

"Rick. What are you doing?"

"Hello, gorgeous." The man stood up and flexed his muscles under the thick coat, for her benefit. God, what a loser.

"Rick, I told Sally this morning that I didn't need any firewood."

His face fell, but then recovered. "I know, but I decided you wouldn't know how much wood you'd need over the next few months. It don't warm up here until July, most years." He suddenly looked young and vulnerable. And somewhat embarrassed.

Delmont felt sorry for him, sorry and irritated. It was probably better not to start a firewood war; she'd take whatever he'd put in the barn.

"Okay, but that's enough, I don't need any more than what you've already put there."

"I hove a load aboard, and here we are — dried birch. I see Bill Grant sold you spruce and juniper. Well, I'm here to tell you, birch burns warmer and cleaner, especially in a fireplace. And there's lots more where this came from."

Delmont sat on the smile. It wouldn't have been the kind he was looking for.

"Do you want a coffee?"

"Got no beer?"

"Don't drink much, so I rarely buy any." That should keep him away. And all the rest of the alcoholics in this place.

They walked into the house together. Delmont put the coffee on and excused herself to go upstairs to change into her jeans. When she came down, Rick had a fire going and was stretched out in front of it. She got two mugs of coffee and took them to the small antique table by the fireplace. She almost sat down beside him—she was drawn to the heat and cheerful crackle of the hearth—but she knew that he would think she was making a move on him. Fat chance, country boy, although he did look good in his sweaty shirt and tight jeans. The male version of his sister. If only he were unable to speak . . .

He looked up at her and smiled. "Excuse me, I may smell. I'm sweatin' like a Beck's Cove Whore."

"Why do the whores of Beck's Cove sweat more than other whores?" she said in a sarcastic voice. Jesus, if only someone had cut out his tongue when he was a baby.

He laughed, and she realized her mistake. He thought she was flirting. She chose the chair on the side of the table farthest away from the fireplace.

"Where's Dave this evening?"

"Oh, he's in the woods cuttin' logs for a new garage he's plannin' on buildin' in the spring. I usually goes in with him, but I had a drunk last night and wasn't up to it."

The smell of his sweat reached her, riding on the scent of

the fire. It was sweet and acrid, like the smoke. She suddenly felt bone-weary and wished she could lie down in front of the fire, with his arms around her. The thought jolted her awake. She had been on the point of dozing off. Time to get him out of here. His mug was empty, anyway.

Standing, she said, "How much do I owe you?"

"Birch is sixty a load, but fifty is good."

Delmont got three twenties from her purse and passed them to Rick.

"I said fifty was enough."

"Take it. You stored it, it's worth sixty."

And there he was, grinning and looking cocky again. "I learned a long time ago not to argue with women." He stuffed the money in his jeans pocket and put on his coat and boots.

"Rick, may I ask you a question?"

"Sure—personal or sexual?"

By the way he was smiling, Delmont figured that sort of thing must pass for the height of wit in Setback. "How old are you?"

"Twenty-two."

"You look older."

"Honey, that's not the first time I heard that."

"Keep drinking the way you drink, you'll look fifty when you're thirty."

Rick scowled and left without saying a word. Delmont watched him run down the steps. He always seemed to move like someone was chasing him. Or he was running towards something he badly wanted, full speed ahead. She liked the way he moved, smooth and feline. Perhaps she might end up having a taste, some cold and lonely night. But the cold didn't bother her, and she was rarely lonely. Touch was good, sometimes, though. That human connection. Although Sally might not like it if she found out. The other thing about Rick was that she could use him as a buffer between herself and the rest of the men in the community. He was irritating but harmless. She went over to the door and checked that it was locked tight.

"Sally, you were going to tell me the rest of the Grant brothers' story." Delmont and the town clerk were taking a break together in the kitchenette in the council building.

"From what I recall, when the police questioned people around town, they soon found out that Gerry Lyver was sleepin' with Walter Grant's wife. When the RCMP went lookin' for Walter, they couldn't find him. Apparently, the night of the murder, he took off and walked in over the ridge to his cabin, ten kilometres from town. Three days later, six Mounties went in on ATVs, with a helicopter overhead for support. There was an eight-hour standoff. Eventually, he walked out of the cabin with his hands in the air. They charged him with second-degree murder, and he was convicted after a twelve-day trial. It took them a few days to find the car and the body. Actually, it was Bill's other brother, Mick, who found them. Some people say he was in on it. So be careful around them Grants."

"Don't worry. Mr. Grant will be seeing Dr. Shandal from now on; he's a better fit. And if I need firewood, there's always Rick."

"I got another story if you want to hear it. About another crime that took place in Setback and the person who did it never got caught."

"I guess. I don't have another patient for an hour or so."

"Okay. Here's the other story. Two years after Walter Grant was locked up, a man named Gill Pond was beaten into a coma out on Powerhouse Road on the north side of town. That's directly across the harbour from where you live. It happened in the spring when the fishermen get together to draw their cod trap berths at the parish hall."

"What are cod trap berths?"

"It's the places where the fishermen put their cod traps along the coast for the summer. Some locations are better than others, which is why they draw for them. To make it fair. So, after this draw, all hands headed to the Longview for a few beers, like they always do. Most years, there's guaranteed to be a fight or two, because some of them aren't satisfied with the berth they got. This draw was two years after Walter was locked up, and there was a major brawl at Longview afterwards. Six men were arrested; two of them were in hospital. One was Rock McGee, the bouncer. He was tryin' to stop the fightin', a couple brothers from the north side of the harbour attacked him. One of the fishermen, Gill Pond, fought three different men and beat all three of them. He was staggerin' home on Powerhouse Road when someone attacked him from behind and beat him with a wooden baseball bat. He's been in a coma in a disability home in St. John's ever since; he can't speak or feed himself. They never found out who did it. He was beaten really bad; he had splinters in his skull from the bat. No charges were ever laid. Setback might seem quiet, but someone is walkin' around out there who tried to kill Gill Pond with a baseball bat."

"Well, Sally, that gives me a new outlook on this quiet little town. How bad was the bouncer beaten?"

"He wasn't, he spent one night in hospital. And when he recovered, he beat the three brothers one on one within weeks. Rock McGee is mean, no one messes with him."

"Well, Sally, interesting stories." Delmont had always had a soft spot for psychopaths. Just not in person. And yet, there seemed to be one in Setback she just might run across, even if she was unaware of his status as a crazy person.

"Yes, they are."

"I have to get back to work, Sally. I'm up to my ears preparing for two group meetings at the parish hall, one on Monday with plant workers and one on Wednesday with fishermen. The Fish Food and Allied Workers union set them up. But are you coming over to help me paint on Saturday?"

"Oh yes, Tish. Like the song says, wild horses couldn't keep me away. I'll bring a bottle of wine, okay?"

Delmont suppressed an exasperated expletive. When had it started, she wondered, the inability of these people to pass a day or night without drinking? "Not for me, Sally. But certainly, for yourself, although you'll be driving of course."

Sally looked crestfallen. "Oh, well, you shouldn't drink by yourself they say. Anyway, it's no fun. You're not religious or nothin', are you? I don't mean to be nosy, but I was wonderin' if you don't like to drink because you were saved or somethin'. Or you're one of them super Catholics like my nan."

"Oh, Sally, no. I have a few drinks from time to time. But the amount of alcohol consumption in Setback is astounding. Alcohol is a poison, essentially; in small amounts, it's therapeutic, possibly, but in the amounts consumed around here, it's very unhealthy, mentally and physically."

Sally looked sullen; that was a new expression for her. She must have her feelings hurt. Well, why not? Delmont had just insulted her people and her own person. She must try to smooth things over.

"I know, Sally, that there's not much to do or see in Setback, and that life is lived very close to the bone. I didn't mean to insult you or your people, I'm just concerned. Professionally and personally."

Sally brightened up. "Oh, Tish, I know you didn't mean nothin' by what you said. You have a different outlook on

Setback, that's all, 'cause you're not from here and you're a shrink."

Delmont laughed a short, sharp bark. "Guilty on both counts. See you tomorrow."

Chapter 9

ON SATURDAY, SALLY WAS AT DELMONT'S RESIDENCE BEFORE
nine. She knocked several times, finally, Delmont arrived at
the door and let her in.

"You look like you were up all night."

Delmont had had a quick glimpse of herself in the mirror
on the wall: she knew she had dark circles under her eyes, and
that her hair was standing up like a rooster's tail.

"Yeah, I was. Not all night, but I put in a lot of work
before I went to bed, and then I had a hard time sleeping. I
really, really miss my dog – she could always put me to sleep
just by snoring next to me."

"Just like Rex!" Sally was smiling when she said his name,
for the first time since Delmont had known her. Well, time
heals all wounds they say. Too bad it took so long for the

healing. She thought briefly about her lawyer and then shook him out of her head.

"Where's the paint and which room first?"

"In the room next to mine. It's nice and small and I'm going to make a study out of it. I don't like working downstairs. It's a little creepy."

"Okay. You go back to bed, and I'll paint the room. I'm a fast painter, I'll have it done in roughly three or four hours."

"I couldn't let you do that, Sally."

"Yes, you can. Go on back to bed, you look terrible."

"Well, now, that's so sweet. I could kiss you." And I really could, thought Delmont. Eat you right up, just like the big bad wolf.

Sally blushed, as was customary for her when just about any random emotion coursed through her pretty veins. "I'll pass. See you in a few hours."

Sally worked away, painting the ten-foot walls with a roller on an extra-long extension pole attached to the roller handle. She did the cut-ins on an eight-foot ladder she found in the basement. She was so engrossed in painting, several hours passed quickly. And then she heard the shower running. Shortly after that, it stopped and a few minutes later Delmont appeared, in jeans and sneakers and a strap shirt.

"How's the painting going?"

"Great, but these ten-foot walls are much harder to paint than eight-foot walls."

Sally was shocked to see what looked like a tattoo on Delmont's right arm. Only sailors and skeets had tattoos.

"Tish, what's that on your arm, if you don't mind me askin'."

"It's a tattoo. A feather. I had a good friend who died; she was part Native American. Choctaw. Her tribal name was Shikoba, which means feather. She was the first one in her family to go to college, smart as a whip. But she wasn't smart enough to beat the alcoholism in her family and the ancestral trauma. That's partly why I became an expert on the things that are affecting your community. She looked a bit like you, Sally, but I could never love another woman the way I loved her. She was my soul." Delmont pushed these thoughts as far away from her as she could and changed the subject. "Sally, I can't thank you enough. You've been so helpful to me since I arrived in Setback. I owe you."

"Don't be so foolish. That's what the people of Setback do. We help each other."

"I'm going to make us some sandwiches. I'm having a BLT. Would you like one?"

"Sure, I'm starved, all that hard work the past few hours."

"What would you like to drink?"

"A glass of milk, if you have any."

"I do. Unless you want Carnation. I understand there's a general antithesis here towards 'cow's milk,' as Bill Grant called it."

Sally smiled. Her teeth were so white and straight you

could film an ad with them, thought Delmont. The rest of her was ad-worthy as well. "Oh, Bill Grant. What does he know? You couldn't get milk back in the day unless you had a cow, so people were used to tinned milk. Carnation. I'd love a big, cold glass of milk. And then I'll get back to the paintin'. I should be finished in a half hour or so. I have to finish the cut-ins on one wall and around the window."

"Can I help?"

"No, you'll only be in my way. More of a hindrance than a help, I work best alone."

"Fine. I was going to get a few groceries. I shouldn't be longer than an hour."

"I'll be finished by then."

When the room had been painted, Sally put the lid on what was left of the paint and washed out the roller and brushes in the bathtub. It was latex paint, so the roller and brushes could be reused. Maybe Tish would want some more painting done. Sally put the painting gear in the basement, and then went upstairs to admire her work one more time. She was pleased with the result and surprised it had only needed two coats to go from powder blue to chestnut brown.

Sally was thirsty. She opened the fridge, craving a beer for thirst. But there was no beer. Maybe she should just have another glass of milk. She was pouring it into a glass when she noticed a nearly empty liquor bottle on the counter. It looked to her like a bottle of red wine, but she'd never seen the name before, Cinzano. She liked Blue Nun, herself.

When Delmont got back with the groceries, she put them away and sat down with Sally at the kitchen table with a cup of coffee.

"So, Tish, what's that like, that Cinzano? It's red wine, right?"

Delmont smiled at the girl's pronunciation of the vermouth brand. *Sinsan-oh*. How cute. "No, Sally, it's vermouth, which is, yes, wine, but wine with a lot of herbs and spices and stuff in it, and alcohol added to it. It's really good with a toke. And it's pronounced Chin-ZAN-o."

Sally looked properly horrified, which was what Delmont had intended. "Tish! *You* smokes up?"

"Yes, Sally. Well, no, not these days. But back in university, I had my share of dope. Only marijuana, though. I had and still have a healthy respect for the downsides of psychedelics. Hey, have you got any plans for tonight? You could come over and have a few drinks, stay over if you get too drunk to drive – and I'll prove to you that I really do have a drink or three sometimes." What was she thinking? What had she said? Oh, hell's bells. Too late to take it back now.

"Well, I wasn't plannin' on doin' nothin' except watchin' a movie on cable. Or readin' my book. I'm halfway through a murder mystery, about a game warden gettin' killed in a small town in Alaska."

Murder mysteries. Some of them weren't too bad, Delmont supposed. But whatever Sally was reading probably wasn't exactly in the Arthur Conan Doyle category. You can't expect beauty and brains to go together always. Although Sally wasn't stupid, just limited by her upbringing and culture. But Shikoba – Ruth, actually – had been beautiful and bright, like a star in the firmament. And not at all limited by her background. But she'd had the advantages of a good school in New York metropolitan North American culture.

"Okay, Tish. If Mom can take Bette, we'll have a sleepover. I haven't had one of those since the fifth grade. Give me a call later, and we'll see if I can make it."

Delmont would stake good money that Sally's Grade 5 sleepover hadn't been a bit like the one she was imagining for them.

Chapter 10

THE PHONE RANG FIVE OR SIX TIMES BEFORE SALLY FINALLY answered. "Hey Sally, Tish here. Did you just wake up?"

"I did. Napped for two hours and was it ever nice."

"So, did you get a sitter for Bette?"

"She's been at Mom's all day and stayin' for the night."

"Great. I'm going to make some spaghetti or chili for later. You choose."

"Spaghetti, I guess. I had chili in St. John's once. Nearly took the mouth off me."

"Oh, mine's not that spicy. But spaghetti it is. See you around nine?"

"Okay." Sally hung up the phone and did a little wiggle. A night out with a friend hadn't been many of those since Bette was born. Since Rex died. Sally pushed the thought of Rex into her mental trash can and went to the bathroom to shower.

Delmont went for a long walk in the cold evening; one star was out, or was it Venus? It comforted her to think that the same moon and the same star or planet or whatever the hell it was - UFO? - were also looking down on her condo back in Chicago. When she got back, she went to the barn for firewood. There was a note on the door. "Me and Mick delivered another load of wood for you. See you soon, Bill." Christ for dinner. Delmont tore the note up and stuffed the pieces in her jacket pocket. No, she wouldn't be seeing him soon. Especially with Mick? Hadn't that been the name of his brother who'd been implicated in a murder? She'd have to get a lock for the barn door.

When Sally came in, she wrinkled her nose. "Tish, what's that funny smell?"

"I don't know, Sally. It could be anything. The girl who does the cleaning hasn't been here for over a week – I think her mother is ill, or something. Might have to get someone else. What does it smell like?"

"Like rotten vegetables."

"Oh, shit – I forgot to put out the compost. It's still there by the back door."

"What's that, compost?"

"It's stuff that's biodegradable – mostly the peels of fruit and vegetables. You save them up and put them in a pile in the backyard and it eventually turns into soil. Great for gardening. It's a way of being environmentally responsible."

Sally gave Delmont a quizzical look. 'You're a queer hand, Tish."

"I guess, I am, Sally. A fish out of water, here in Setback."

Sally put her hand on Delmont's shoulder. "I never meant to hurt your feelin's, Tish. You just have ways that are different from ours, that's all. I mean, we're all the same under the skin, aren't we?"

"You didn't hurt my feelings, Sally. You couldn't." Delmont put her hand on top of Sally's and marvelled at its small bones. She resisted the urge to run her hand down Sally's arm. And elsewhere. "Come sit down, and I'll pour you a drink. Are you hungry?"

"No, Mom had supper made when I got home. A big pot of pea soup."

They sat and sipped, travelling through the few topics they could talk about – local gossip, the weather, men. Delmont was starting to worry about running out of conversation. She supposed she could always get Sally back on the topic of Rex and let the girl get worn out with crying. Worn out and ready for bed. And then Sally said, "Tish, I have a suggestion. There's an Irish Newfoundland band playin' at Longview tonight called Alley Road. They're from Bay Bulls, on the Southern Shore. Why don't we go over and have a few scuffs?"

"Scuffs? Scuffles? You want us to fight?" Oh, dear Lord in fishnets, what next?

Sally burst out laughing and choked on her wine. Between

coughs, she said. "No, Tish, a scuff is a dance. You got to hear this band – Rick says they're really good. You've never heard any Irish music, have you?"

"Sally, of course I have. Chicago is full of Irish pubs. In fact, I once dated a bodhran player."

"If he was borin', why did you date him?"

Now it was Delmont's turn to laugh. "No, Sally, not boring, *bodhran*. That's the name of the Irish drum."

"Oh, I'm so stunned, Tish. I never knew that. So, you want to go to Longview, or what?"

Delmont would rather have a root canal, but she knew that Sally was tied down with her child most of the time and needed some fun. Besides, it would be an expedition, some cultural anthropology. She would get a better feel for her patients if she saw them in their native habitat, at their watering hole. "Sure, why not? But just for an hour or so, okay?"

Sally's face shone like the star planet - Delmont had seen earlier. "Great! I'll call Rick to come get us, and if we don't hook a run back, we can grab a cab."

"No, Sally. Rick told me he's never sober on a Saturday."

"Well, he's sober today. Got a really bad case of the flu and never drank a beer since Wednesday."

"Will he want to drive us if he's not feeling well?"

"Oh sure. He went to the store for Mom today, he's not that bad now."

Sally called Rick and he agreed to pick them up at ten-thirty. Delmont looked at her watch. Half an hour. Surely, she could keep the conversation going that long. "Tell me about your family, Sally. All of it, as far back as you know anything."

There was a knock at the door. Delmont was startled; she had been so engrossed in Sally's family saga that she'd forgotten all about going out. What a lot of – colourful – characters. Certifiable, half of them.

"Come in, Rick. We're just putting our coats and boots on."

"Hello, sweetheart. Don't bother offerin' me a beer. I'm on antibiotics and I can't drink."

"Oh, what a shame, afraid you might get pregnant?"

Rick scowled at her. The sarcasm was not lost on Sally's brother.

When they arrived at the club, the parking lot was full of vehicles. Delmont's heart made a run for her expensive new boots. She'd just remembered the nickname of the joint: The Swamp.

When they walked through the door, Delmont could feel that every set of eyes in the club were on them. She shrugged. That was par for the course in a tiny place like this. A woman they had never seen before – she would have the wow factor, all right. The guy collecting the cover fee at the door was big and not bad looking. And his eyes were as dim as a sheep in the field. She figured him for the famous Rock Someone-or-Other, bouncer, that Sally had mentioned. And he was more like a rock than a sheep, she decided. Big and dumb and slow. Except in a fight, probably.

As soon as the two women had their coats off, they were swarmed by dance partners. Delmont reflected it was good she'd had all that training in Irish bars in her hometown, or she'd have had all her toes broken here tonight. And no one would let them buy themselves drinks. The local men paid for their wine. There was no vermouth in Setback, except the two bottles she'd found in the liquor store, apparently.

"Who's your good-lookin' friend, Sally?"

"This is Tish Delmont, Walter. Tish, this is Walter Grant, Bill's brother. And that's Mick, Bill's other brother."

Delmont glanced up at the two men looming over their table. They looked a bit like Bill, but Mick had a more simian appearance. "Hello, Walter. Yes, I've met your brother."

Walter grinned. Leered. "Yeah, he told us about the hot piece of ass livin' out on South Side Point Road. Want to dance?'

Delmont looked him straight in the eyes, making sure he could see the contempt in them. "No thanks. We were just getting ready to leave, weren't we, Sally?" Out of the corner of her eye, she could see the disappointment on Sally's face. She felt sorry for the girl, but it was time to go. It had been time to go since they'd walked in the door, in her opinion. If only she could take Sally away, show her what life could be like. When she went back to Chicago, she'd probably feel as though she'd left a lamb to the slaughter. But it was the girl's culture; her mother had survived it, and she would too. A pity, though.

"I'm goin' to ask Rock for a run home, Tish."

"Is he sober, do you think?"

"He might have had a couple of beers, but he'd lose his job if he has more than that. Old Man Watts, the guy who owns the bar, is strict about his staff drinkin'. One time one of his barmaids got so drunk she spewed all over the bar and he come in and poured a whole jugful of water on her and threw her out the door. In the dead of winter and everythin'. She never even had her coat on."

Delmont realized she would never have to visit the Ozarks, as much as she loved to travel. This place was close enough.

Two hours later, Delmont found herself next to the bouncer in the cab of his pickup. He took every chance he got to "accidentally" touch her leg when he was changing gears. That wasn't as bad as having to breathe in his aftershave. Had no one told these guys that aftershave was passé? She was tempted to send out the memo on Monday.

After about a thousand years, in Delmont's estimation, the truck turned down the road to her house. As he pulled up to the door, Rock looked as if he were expecting an invite to join them inside.

"Well, thanks very much, Rock. You know, I think the ride home was the most enjoyable part of the whole evening."

Rock, unable to see the joke, flexed his biceps and looked smug. Surely, he wasn't going to show up at her door with a load of wood too. She seemed to be – quite innocently – on her way to being the cause of an ecological disaster – by the time she left, there wouldn't be a tree standing in Setback.

The next hour was spent eating spaghetti and salad and garlic bread, and then drinking water and taking Aspirin, to fend off any potential hangovers. Although both had drunk more than they intended to, they had danced it off.

"Walter Grant looks like a mean guy, Sally. And his brother is positively simian – I mean, he looks like a monkey."

Sally giggled. "That used to be Mick's nickname at school. Chimp. And Walter is mean. Ever since the Lyver murder, almost everyone in town avoids the Grants."

"Well, I guess I will too. Sally, I'm tired now – if you want to stay up, go right ahead, but I'm going to have to turn in. But before I do, I'll get you some sheets and a pillow for the couch. For some reason, none of the other rooms have beds. Or much furniture at all."

"Oh, I guess the Squires kids took all that after their parents died. None of them wanted the house, and they haven't been able to sell it." Sally looked uncertainly at Delmont. "Tish, I hate to ask, but can I sleep with you? I don't like the idea of sleepin' down here on me own – as you said, it's kind of creepy."

Oh, dear God. *And lead us not into temptation but deliver us from evil.* Well, it was unlikely the Lord's Prayer was going to save her now. Willpower would, though. And exhaustion.

"Sure thing, Sally. You go on up to bed; I'm going to soak in the bath for a while. Get the Swamp out of my skin."

"I know how you feel, Tish. But I'm too tired to take a shower. I'll probably be asleep by the time you get in bed."

With any luck, thought Delmont. She decided to stay in the old claw-foot bathtub for a long time.

Someone was calling Delmont's name from a long way off. She thought it might be her mother; but what was she doing in her mother's house? Her mother was visiting London with her best friend, Dolly. And she, she wasn't in Chicago either. She was in the Outback. No, that wasn't right. Not Australia, Canada. Setback. And then she woke up fully, to a bathtub full of tepid water and a knocking on the bathroom door.

"Tish, are you all right?"

The girl sounded frightened. She probably thought she was going to have to deal with a drowned corpse. "Sally – yes, I'm fine. I just dozed off, I guess. I'll be out in a minute." Delmont climbed out of the tub, shivering, and grabbed a towel. She dried herself off, wrapped a big, clean towel around her cold body, and went to her bedroom.

Sally looked relieved to see her. "I thought somethin' might have happened to you." The girl turned her head as Tish took out clean panties and a T-shirt and put them on.

A Victorian table lamp with wrought iron jaguars and a red, glass shade was the only illumination in the bedroom; Delmont thought how pretty Sally looked, sitting up in bed beside it. A southerly wind was rapping against the house. Delmont suddenly felt so tired she was afraid she'd just lie down and go to sleep on the floor. But she managed to slide in beside the girl and pull up the sheets and quilts and the eiderdown.

"Oh bed, I love you so much."

Sally turned and smiled at Delmont. "I say the same thing any night that I crawl in bed exhausted."

"I've wanted to kiss you since the first day I saw you." Who said that – it couldn't have been her, God please no. "Oh, hell, Sally, I didn't mean it. I'm so tired I don't know what I'm saying. Go to sleep." Delmont moved to the far side of the bed, near the window. The wind was howling now, and she felt like howling along with it. And then she felt Sally's hand on her back.

"Tish, it's all right. I thought you might be a lesbian. Rick and them were sayin' you was. They said you didn't like men; they could tell by the way you were treatin' them. Only I'm not a lesbian. Do you want me to go down and sleep on the couch? I don't mind. I'm that tired, I'll go right to sleep, ghosts or no ghosts."

Bless the child. Delmont sighed and sat up. "I'm not a lesbian, Sally. But I did have one affair with a woman. 'Affair' is not the right word: I loved her more than I have ever loved another human being or ever will. And you look so much like her."

Sally was sitting up now and looking far from sleepy. "I

do? That's wild, Tish. Do you want to tell me about it? I mean, you've been so good about listenin' to me goin' on about Rex and everythin'. I'd be more than happy for you to tell me about – the girl you loved. But only if you want to."

To her surprise, Delmont found that she did want to. "I went to a college out east – Smith, it's called – it's in Massachusetts. It's one of the most prestigious colleges in the US, and it's for women only. I was there on a merit scholarship, and so was she. It costs a lot of money to attend Smith, and there's no way my mother or her parents could have afforded the tuition. But we both were smart enough to get scholarships, and we each had grants as well, and worked during the summers and saved money."

Delmont took a deep breath. This was hard, but not too hard. Sally's quiet presence and the sad wind and the old house made it seem right, somehow. "I first saw Ruth in an English lecture, the first week I was at Smith. She was bent over her notes, scribbling away. Her hair was so thick and black, hanging down in the back in a big braid. I could tell she was at least part native, and I guess I stared a little too long at her because the next thing you know she turned around and made a face at me. I burst out laughing, and then everyone looked at me. Especially the prof. But she waited for me after class – Ruth, not the prof – and -"

"What's a prof?"

"Sorry – a professor. Teacher. Anyway, I thought she was waiting to chew me out, but no – she just wanted to go for a coffee and to pick my brains about Shakespeare. It was an introductory Shakespeare course. And that was it. We hung around every spare minute we weren't chasing guys. We hiked and skated and drank and studied and managed to get rooms in the same dorm – dormitory, it's a building full of rooms for students – and we even planned a vacation together. But just before the spring term ended, she got word that her oldest brother, Jonas, had died of a drug overdose. There was a lot of addictive behaviour in her extended family owing to generations of trauma, but her own family had been clean until Jonas. She left and went home to be with her family, and when she came back in the fall she had changed."

"You weren't friends anymore, Tish?"

"We were still friends, Sally; we were closer than ever, actually. I used to think it was too bad she wasn't a guy because I'd have married her on the spot. No, we were close, it's just that she had lost her spirit, her confidence. She was clingy and needy, but I figured she'd come around in time. She and Jonas were close; the whole family was close. They were suffering something awful over her brother's death. Blaming themselves. Guilt is always a part of death, even when it doesn't need to be. Ruth blamed herself terribly; Jonas had confided in her about his drug-taking and his depression, but she hadn't taken him seriously. She figured it was just a stage because he'd always been upbeat and easygoing, just like her.

Anyway, one night I went into her room, and she was sitting there moaning and rocking and there was blood running down her arms. She'd cut herself. I didn't know what to do, I was so afraid. She didn't seem able to take in anything I was saying to her, so finally, I just shoved her into her bed, got in beside her and held her. And we ended up making love."

Sally's eyes were as big as the lenses of Delmont's reading glasses sitting on the night table. "Go *on*. What was it like?"

Delmont chewed on her lip. "I don't know. It was strange, but it was beautiful. And afterwards, we were . . . well, we were a couple, not officially, not in front of other people. But we were a couple, a couple in love. And she, Ruth, she seemed to get better. I was going to take her home to Chicago that Christmas, but –"

Delmont's face was running with tears, and her voice was shaky. "But she drowned in the Mill River, it's a river by the college. And I never knew if she did it on purpose or if it was an accident. She was a good swimmer, Sally, I can't see how it was an accident . . ."

Delmont was sobbing now. Sally moved over and put her arms around her. "It's okay, Tish, it's all right. I'm so sorry, I am." The two women clung together, tears running down both their faces.

And then Sally said, "You know, Tish, you can kiss me if you want, I don't mind."

Delmont touched the soft full lips with her own and shivered. She turned her head.

"What's wrong, Tish?"

"Sally, you are a lovely person, but you aren't Ruth, as

much as you look like her. And she was the only woman I could ever imagine loving."

Sally brushed the tears off Delmont's face with her hand. "Well, what about we get some sleep then, Tish? Unless you want to talk some more."

"No, Sally, I don't want to talk about Ruth ever again, to anyone. It's too painful. But I think I needed that cry. It's hard for me being in a strange place without my family or my friends sometimes."

Delmont turned the light off. They lay down in the dark and fell asleep curled up together, while the wind shrieked, and the cold moon looked indifferently at them through the window.

———————————

Chapter 11

———————————

When Delmont arrived at the office, Sally wasn't in.
She wondered why; Sally was always in before her. Perhaps
Bette had made her late. She hoped the child wasn't ill. Sally
was fierce about her one chick, and she worried too much.

Noon rolled around and Delmont ate lunch alone in the
kitchenette. She liked eating alone, it was easier to appreciate
the food. That was the trick for not gaining weight: eat like a
Buddhist. Savour every mouthful and stop eating when your
body tells you it's had enough.

When she arrived at the parish hall for her first group
meeting, she was shocked by how old and weathered the
building looked but pleased with the number of vehicles in the
yard.

Inside, there were roughly forty people, with a fifty-fifty
mix of males and females, sitting in small groups of three and

four spread out over the large hall. She walked to the table at the front of the room, where the president of the Fish, Food and Allied Workers Union, Ray Rashin, and a few men from the union's executive were waiting for her. She took the microphone and asked the crowd in the hall to move to the front so that they could hear her. Most of them moved; she introduced herself and gave her credentials.

She explained the reason for the meeting to the plant workers: that she had felt not all of them would want to see a psychologist individually. Perhaps they felt uncomfortable with the idea, or maybe they were afraid others in the community would find out and look down on them. "But there is nothing to be ashamed of. All over the world, people just like you are suffering from the loss of industries they had depended on for work for what they thought would be their entire lives. And this is just a moratorium; you could be back in the plant sooner than you think." A cheer went up, punctuated by some whistling.

"In the meantime, the federal government is taking good care of you – you are being given some income, and are eligible for training in new trades, free of charge. If you have to go to the city to do that, they will pay for travel and lodging. Through my work, I have seen similar situations play out. You in Canada are lucky with your socialist government; I don't know if you appreciate what you have here. In many, many other parts of the world, when industries go under, there is no help, not even social assistance programs."

So, since your government is willing to give you a hand, why don't you return the favour? Stay positive, stay away from drugs and heavy drinking, keep busy, and consider your options, just in case. And if things get too hard to handle, come see me. There's no shame in going for help if your brain is giving you trouble. It's just another organ in the body, like the liver or the pancreas or the heart. I'm sure a few of you here today are taking medication for your heart, or for diabetes. Well, I can get you some medication for your brain, if the need arises. And if I can't help you, I can get you in to see a Doctor in St. John's."

Someone called out from the back: "Sure Jimmy Woodward he'll never need any of them pills, 'cause he got no brain!"

There was a howl of laughter from the crowd. That was good; they were relaxed, and, Delmont hoped, receptive.

"Does anyone have any questions?"

A middle-aged man strode to the table and took the microphone out of her hand.

"This is the goddamn prime minister's and federal fisheries minister's fault. They bargained away our fish, so foreign countries would buy wheat from the prairies and iron ore from Ontario. They hung us out to dry. Ottawa has screwed us since '49 and will screw us as long as we can survive on this rock. I say, fuck the federal government!"

Everyone in the hall got to their feet and roared and

clapped. As the man walked back to his seat, many people tapped him on the back or shook his hand.

The union president took the mike. "We will keep this civil. This is no way to get on in front of Dr. Delmont. She'll think we're a crowd of savages."

Out of the corner of her eye, Delmont saw a bald, red-faced man approaching the table. He grabbed the mike from the FFAW official and glared at him.

"The fuckin' FFAW is no better than the fuckin' federal government, and you as president have been in bed with the federal fisheries department for too long. Our union has been silent for too long. The only good thing with the collapse of the cod fishery is that the union will collapse as well, and every cocksucker that works for it gets the same paycheck we gets every two weeks. "

The roar from the crowd was louder than the surf outside the window of the house on South Side Point Road. The sound finally subsided, and the crowd moved as one towards the door, shouting obscenities at the union president and the members of the executive as they went.

Well, that was interesting. They certainly were a united bunch, thought Delmont. That was a plus for them, something to ground them in bad times.

The FFAW president apologized to Delmont for what had happened. "A lot of people have a lot of issues, and they need to vent. Unfortunately, myself and the union were the targets today."

Delmont looked sympathetic or tried to. "Oh, it's quite normal for people to show their frustration like that. It's a very hard time for them."

The man looked at her and scratched his head. "Wednesday could be rougher, Dr. Delmont. It will be all fishermen, no women, and a few of them are known drinkers. I expect them to show up with liquor in them, and less civil than the crowd that was just here. I'm going to request that an RCMP officer be present."

Delmont thanked him for setting up the meetings. As she was about to head back to the office, the manager of the fish plant introduced himself and offered to take her on a tour of the plant. She told him she would love to see the plant and hoped that he'd forget that he'd asked her. She crossed her fingers.

When Delmont pulled into the parking lot of the parish hall on Wednesday afternoon, an RCMP cruiser was parked close to the door. With any luck, it would be Terry Ross.

There were fewer people in the hall this time. The RCMP officer was at the front of the hall, standing so that the crowd could see him, but not front and center so that his presence would be an irritant to them. Well, he was a professional, after all.

When she asked the fishermen to move to the front, they sat silently where they were. There seemed to be two groups, ten or twelve men on each side of the hall. She smiled and shrugged and made the same speech to them as she had made to the plant workers.

A grey-haired, weathered man stood up abruptly in the middle of it and said, "The government should take care of us, they're the ones who put us on handouts."

Ray Rashin, the union president, looked less than comfortable. "No comments or questions until after the meeting."

This was greeted with snickering. Delmont ploughed on, reminding them that alcohol was a depressant.

A voice shouted: "We'd be pretty fuckin' depressed if we didn't have it."

The crowd roared with laughter. Delmont felt like a fifth-grade teacher. If only she could send a few of them to the principal.

"And street drugs and negative people are just as bad as booze." This time a young man decided to bless the gathering with what passed for wit among adult men in Setback.

"My wife depresses me, so I tries my best to stay away from her. Spends most of my time out in the shed, I does."

Mentally, Delmont downgraded them to the fourth grade. But they couldn't help being so limited. She tried to feel sorry for them and failed. "You need to keep busy, physically and mentally active. Walking, cutting firewood, hunting, whatever it takes to get a good night's sleep. And watch what you eat; a balanced diet contributes to good physical and mental health."

Another local comedian got his two cents worth in. "We'll all be as thin as Lazarus in a few years."

"Any questions?" She half expected someone to ask when recess was, but no, the young man with the depressing wife was getting to his feet. He looked pretty depressed himself. And angry.

"This is Mulrooney and Crosbie's fault; they gave away our fish. There are at least twenty foreign trawlers on the Grand Banks every day of the week, there now as we speak, and the federal government won't do a goddamn thing about it. They're nothin' but a bunch of cowards. Every cocksucker in Ottawa is gutless. I say fuck the federal government, let's separate. But it's not only the feds, the provincial government's a bunch of gutless wonders. They've never opened their mouths to Ottawa; whatever Ottawa says, our provincial fisheries minister agrees with - he won't butt heads with Ottawa."

The men on the right side of the hall, the side the young man was sitting on, stood, clapped, and yelled. Not one person on the left side of the hall made a sound.

Rashin stood. "We'll keep this civil; this is no way to get on in front of Dr. Delmont. Dr. Delmont is not up on Canadian politics. She was good enough to come here from Chicago to help us work through what we've been dealt."

Delmont started to thank the people for coming, but she was interrupted by another angry young man. "The fuckin' union is no better than the federal government. You, the union president, have gone along with the federal fisheries department for way too long. Our union has been quiet for too long. The only good thing I sees with the collapse of the cod fishery is that if the fish come back, there'll be no fishermen's union."

Everyone on both sides clapped and cheered. There was enthusiastic foot stomping. Delmont glanced at Terry Ross, who was now standing at the door of the hall. She thought she'd caught his eye, but his face remained impassive. Jesus in short pants, he could be a poster boy for the RCMP.

She tried to speak again, to thank the crowd, but they had already gotten to their feet and were starting to leave. The group on the right side of the hall, followed a couple of minutes later by the group on the left. Ross followed the second group outside.

Rashin looked weary. "Dr. Delmont, it was so good of you to do this today."

"Just part of the job, really."

"I'm sorry you had to be subjected to all that, but you can't blame them for their anger."

"I'm curious. Why were there two groups here today? I thought they'd be a single unit. But they seemed quite separate."

Rashin sighed. "Religion, I'm afraid. One of those groups was Catholic, one Protestant. They live separately in this area, and they vote separately. The Protestants tend to vote Liberal and the Catholics Conservative. Liberal and

Conservative are roughly equivalent to Democrat and Republican."

"Are you serious?"

"Yes."

"I've read several books on Northern Ireland. But never in my life did I think I would experience seeing it."

"On St. Stephens Day known now as Boxing Day. In 1883, in Harbour Grace, which is in Conception Bay. When the Orangeman's Lodge was holding their annual march through town. Catholics from a nearby town Riverhead confronted them, five men were killed and seventeen injured. And not one person served a day in jail over it. It's called the Harbour Grace Affray. Worth looking up."

"I will. Thanks for telling me about it. People live in tribes of some sort all over the world. It's an inherent part of human nature, and our tribal influences have more of an impact on us than we'd like to believe. Not a very good impact sometimes."

"That's very true."

"Well, Ray, to change the subject, the main thing that's come out of this meeting for me is that, as I already knew, a lot of people here are angry and frustrated with the system and what they've been dealt. Now, anger isn't a bad thing – it's strong and empowering. Depression is what kills people. So, I might have to tell them to burn down the union office at some point, if I think they're giving up and at risk of self-harm."

Ray Rashin looked shocked, and then his face relaxed and he laughed. "You had me there for a second, Tish."

"There hasn't been a case of suicide for a few months, now, which might be a statistical blip or might be of some significance. I've seen a lot of patients, and I intend to see a lot more. I'm available twenty-four hours a day all week long. The RCMP and both hospitals, the cottage hospital in Black Tree and the hospital in Gander, have my home number in case of an overnight emergency."

When Delmont left the building, she saw Ross standing by his cruiser having a cigarette. She smiled at him and said, "That's an awful habit."

Ross made a wry face, dropped the remaining three-quarters of his cigarette under his boot and stubbed it out. "I concur. I've been trying to quit for some time."

Delmont reached out and squeezed his arm. 'I know. It's harder than heroin to quit, according to medical research. I only just managed it myself three years ago. But that's not what I meant to say. I was going to ask if you'd like to come out with Sally and me on Saturday night for something to eat."

Ross seemed to be standing straighter. Delmont thought that if he were a dog, his ears would be pricked right up.

"Sure thing. Let me treat you two. Why don't we have Chinese food? Hong's is pretty good."

"I've heard that. I'll see if Sally's okay with that. And as for paying, I'll stick it on my expense account. You can fill me in on anything that's pertinent to my professional duties here. And you can fill me in on anything impertinent as well." She gave him her biggest smile, although she knew she didn't have to. Anywhere Sally would be, he didn't have to be coaxed into being there too. And as for Sally's food preferences, the girl would eat dirt out of a spoon if Terry Ross was feeding it to her.

"Sounds great." Ross was grinning like the fool he was. Not that he was a fool in general, but everyone was a fool for love, as the song said.

"I have to run. See you Saturday evening."

"Yes, ma'am. Looking forward to it."

As Delmont drove away, she thought about the meeting she had just left. A rough group of men, most with little education. Shackled from birth to one kind of life. But that brutal life had made them tougher than most people. And it was a healthy life or would be if they would lay off the booze and cigarettes.

When she returned to the office, Sally was gone for the day. She would phone her when she got back home after she went for a run. She looked out the window: great flakes of snow were beginning the dance that usually led to a storm sooner or later. Or perhaps it would just be a squall, although the sky was leaden as far as she could see.

Later, after she ate and washed the few things she had used, she called Sally to tell her she was going to St. John's the next day for a meeting with her committee members. And to tell the girl about their date with Terry Ross.

From the sound of Sally's voice, Delmont knew the girl was pleased about Ross. She was probably beet red and having trouble holding the phone in her trembling hands. Oh well, being caught up in a romantic soap opera wasn't the worst thing Delmont had ever experienced. Not by a long shot.

"He suggested eating at the Chinese place – would that suit you?"

"Suit me? I'd eat dirt if I was eatin' it with him."

"That's what I figured. I'll call him and tell him it's a go. See you Saturday."

Poor Sally. Delmont knew that although she had a crush on Ross, the girl was ambivalent about a relationship with him. For one thing, she was still grieving Bette's father. Grief had its own timeline; you couldn't make it a shorter process without damage to the psyche. Also, from a few things Sally had let drop, she was worried about what a future with the RCMP officer might entail. Moving out of Setback, of course, and then moving more than once after that. RCMP officers were deployed right across Canada, from the Pacific to the Atlantic. Sally was not the adventuresome type, but her real problem was that she had never met a man she could trust. A sober, grown-up man, who would take responsibility for a woman and a child. She probably had no idea they existed, in any practical sense. And then there was a problem with self-confidence. Sally knew she was pretty, and attractive to men, but she had no idea of her self-worth as a person. That had its roots in her childhood in Setback. Rural children in Newfoundland were fed and kept clean, but they seemed to get no individual attention, from what Delmont had observed.

They were rarely read to or spoken to about their emotions or likes and dislikes. Never spoken to intimately, in fact. Never taken to museums or parks or skating rinks or restaurants. Very little if any travelling outside the province unless it was for work. It was a basic tribal upbringing, sufficient in its way as far as the culture was concerned. Women were expected to cook and clean and breed, and those three things were the bars that kept them in their cages in Setback. Sally lacked confidence in herself and the wider world because she had no knowledge of either.

The drive to St. John's was uneventful but dreary. At one point, Delmont would have cut off at least half a toe just for the sight of a house. But the long, dull Trans Canada Highway snaked along among the forests and barrens and glacial landscape of a country that seemed to have no inhabitants. She was glad when the lights of St. John's came into view. Small as it was, it was a vibrant place. It was an outpost of civilization, the only one in the province.

The meeting on Friday went well and ended early. She told them she believed she was making progress in Setback, among the plant workers at least. Not many fishermen had come to see her, but that was a work in progress. At least she hoped it was.

There was a hint of spring in the air as Delmont walked

along Water Street, purported to be the oldest street in North America. It certainly looked as if it might be. The buildings were old and dingy, crowded into a relatively short stretch lining the harbour. The place smelled old, somehow. But there were lots of places to eat and drink, and she managed to find a restaurant that wouldn't have been out of place in Chicago. The city had a European air that appealed to her. She had always found Europe to her liking during the few trips she had taken there. Must be the ghosts of her Austrian ancestors singing in her blood. Or the English ones on her mother's side.

Her hotel was downtown, so she decided to go for a run up Signal Hill, a steep incline on the city's eastern side made famous by Marconi. On December 12, 1901, he had sent the first wireless transatlantic signal overseas to Cornwall, England. What an earthshaking event to happen in such a tiny, remote place. The run through the narrow streets and the cold wind up the bare hillside was cathartic; she felt like she had shucked a tight carapace. Setback was difficult, but not quite impossible. Looking out over the grey Atlantic, she wondered about all the sailors down through the centuries who had done the impossible: travelled thousands of miles in small ships in search of the fish that had once been as plentiful around this island as ants at a picnic. How sad it was, the collapse of this island's fishery.

Chapter 12

THE THREE-AND-A-HALF-HOUR DRIVE GOT DELMONT BACK TO Setback by noon on Saturday. She was almost glad to see the house on South Side Point Road; it was the closest thing she had to a home north of Chicago, after all. She unpacked, did some reading, and then decided to go for a run.

The wind was cold, colder than it was in St. John's. But she was dressed for it and running pumped the blood through her body until she felt overheated in her fleece jacket, toque, and mittens. She slowed down to a walk to cool off, which didn't take long with the snarling wind of the icy water biting at her exposed face. She was just about to start running again when a truck slowed down beside her. She glanced up and saw Rock McGee leering down at her. Oh, for Christ's sake. Welcomed back by the local thug. One of them, anyway.

McGee rolled his window down. "How're you doin', sweetheart? Pretty cold day to be out traipsin' around – want a ride home?"

She looked at him without a hint of a smile, and replied in a monotone: "No thanks, I'm out for a run, as you can see."

He looked at her as though he was half thinking about getting out of the truck and slapping her around, but only half. "Suit yourself, Yank," he growled and spun gravel at her.

Delmont closed her eyes until he was well down the road. She felt exhausted, suddenly, which was unusual. She was hoping the run would give her energy the way it usually did, but the long drive and the encounter with McGee trumped the run, apparently. She would have to have a nap before she went out with Sally and Terry Ross tonight.

She woke to the sound of the phone ringing downstairs. By the time she got to it, it had stopped ringing. Then it began again.

"Hey Tish, all ready for our date?"

Delmont was still half asleep; it took her a second or two to recognize Sally's voice. "Oh, hi, Sally. Sorry, I'm half asleep."

"When did you get home from St. John's?"

Home? As if. "Arrived back around noon, went for a run and then fell into bed. Didn't expect to sleep so long. What time is it, anyway?"

"Four-thirty. Get on the ball and get yourself dolled up."

"I will, but dinner's not until six-thirty. I'll pick you up, will I?"

"Six-thirty? I'll be starved to death by then. We usually eat supper at five around here."

Delmont could hear her mother's voice in her head. 'Dinner is always eaten after six; anyone who eats before that is a peasant.' "Sorry, Sally, but we keep different mealtimes in Chicago. Anyway, I told Terry to meet us there at six-thirty."

"That's okay, my dear – I'll see you around quarter after six."

Delmont had a long, leisurely bath. She loved the old claw-foot bathtub, its length and curves matched hers. Afterwards, she examined her wardrobe and chose a pair of good jeans, ankle boots and the sweater she had bought in Sweden that time. She still had an hour to kill, and she murdered it by calling a couple of friends. She was more starved for news from home than a meal of Chinese food. Or any other kind.

At quarter after six, she pulled up in front of the small white bungalow with green trim beside the Anglican Church where Sally lived. She parked the car and went to the door. Her hand was poised to knock when the door opened. Apparently, Sally had been watching for her.

"You didn't have to come to the door, Tish. You could have just burmp the horn."

"Yes, well, my mother told me never to do that even if I was choking to death behind the wheel."

"Oh, yeah? I guess that's another Chicago thing, is it?"

"Yup." Nope. It was what civilized people did, but Delmont would cut out her tongue rather than say that to the girl and hurt her feelings. Sally was lit up like a Christmas tree. She probably glowed in the dark if you wanted to experiment with that. Delmont wished she could have been in charge of making the girl up and dressing her, though. She looked as pretty as a picture, but it was kind of a garish one. Too much makeup, too much cleavage, too short a skirt. Oh well, she thought, Sally has enough character and natural dignity to overcome that outfit.

When they got to the restaurant, Terry Ross was standing beside his grey jeep, smoking. When he saw Delmont's car pull up, he threw away the cigarette and sauntered over, smiling. The two women got out and walked to meet him.

"Good evening, ladies. You sure look nice, you two. I guess I should have worn a tie."

"Oh no, Terry, you look great. Different to what you do in your uniform, and different to what you did that day we went for a drive." Sally suddenly stopped talking and turned pink.

Ross squeezed her arm. "Oh, that day, Sally. Well, since then I've had a birthday and my mother sent me this sweater. She said it matches my eyes."

Delmont looked at his eyes: they were almost sapphire; they were such a brilliant blue. You could get hypnotized by those eyes if you weren't careful. Sally obviously hadn't been careful.

Ross held the restaurant door open, and they entered. How alike all Chinese restaurants are, thought Delmont. The jade plant, the lucky red cat, the dragon paraphernalia. It soothed her soul. She could be home in Chicago right now. The place was packed, it was a good thing they had made reservations.

A young Chinese girl came with menus. She asked them if they'd like anything to drink.

"Crown Royal and ginger ale, please."

"A Tom Collins for me."

"Vermouth on the rocks with a twist." Delmont had a feeling she wasn't going to get far with that order, and she was right. The waitress shrugged and said they didn't have any of whatever it was she wanted.

"Okay, then. I guess I'll have a beer. A local beer, maybe Black Horse."

After the waitress left, Sally shot a troubled look at Delmont. "Tish, Black Horse isn't for ladies."

Delmont looked at her in surprise. "Why?"

"I don't know. It just isn't."

Delmont could feel the devil rising in her. "Well, Sally, I'm going to order one and find out why. When I travel, I usually try a local beer or two. If I start growing a beard right here at the table, you let me know, okay?"

Sally looked hurt. Delmont felt a twinge of remorse and tried to repair the damage. "It's just another Chicago thing, Sally. Women and men drink the same things there."

"No, Tish, it can't hurt you or nothin'. But someone might see you and start talking, that's all."

Delmont groaned inwardly. The child was out in public dressed like a hooker and was worried about someone seeing her friend drinking a 'man's beer.' God bless the child. "Don't worry, Sally. I've got a thick skin." She looked at Ross out of the corner of her eye. He was grinning in amusement. Of course, he was like her, he wasn't from a place that had men's beer and "ladies" beer, but he had also been in Setback long enough to know the local dos and don'ts. She should talk with him more often; he could probably help her get a better handle on the place. Idly, she glanced around the restaurant. The Grant brothers, Walter, and Mick were sitting at a table not far from theirs; she quickly averted her gaze, but not before she noted that they were staring fixedly at Sally, Terry, and her. Not a pleasant stare. She moved her eyes towards the door just in time to see Rock McGee come in. Next time she decided to go out to eat, she'd change her mind.

Sally noticed McGee and waved. "Hi, Rock!"

There was no response. Perhaps he hadn't heard her; Delmont fervently hoped so. But she had a feeling he had. She watched him pay for his bag of takeout and leave. The air felt lighter when he'd gone.

The meal was reasonably good, but the menu was limited. Apparently, from what Sally was saying, almost everyone in Setback ordered chicken fried rice, sweet and sour chicken balls and chow mein when they had Chinese food. Although it wasn't Chinese food; Delmont pushed thoughts of her trip to San Francisco's Chinatown out of her mind and ate her Setback Chinese meal.

Halfway through the meal, Delmont saw the Grant brothers leaving. Ross noticed her noticing.

"Bad lot, those two."

"Yes, I heard."

"Tish, did you notice how they stared at us? Never cracked a smile or waved, or nothin'. Maybe they didn't like it that we were havin' dinner with a cop." Sally's head whipped around in Ross's direction. The colour was travelling up her cheeks. "I mean policeman, Terry, I –"

Ross put his hand on top of hers. "That's okay, Sally. You were only saying what they were thinking."

"So, Terry, have you ever had any professional dealings with the Grants? You don't have to give us any of the details, just a yes or no will do. I know you can't divulge those." And I really don't care anyway, Delmont thought.

Ross looked grim. "Yes, I have. And I will give you the details, but I need you to swear you won't tell a soul what I'm about to tell you two."

The two women put their hands over their hearts and promised not to breathe a word. Ross relaxed a little.

"The RCMP is keeping an eye on Walter and Mick. We have reason to believe that the brothers have a poaching ring on the go. Could be as many as six people involved in it. Killing upwards of twenty moose and caribou a year. The department of wildlife is keeping a close eye on them as well. We think they're also out jigging codfish, which is, of course, not allowed with the moratorium in place. The fisheries department and the Coast Guard have been monitoring the coastline day and night, with binoculars and high-powered spotting scopes. So far, no one has been able to catch them.

Also, I hauled the three of them in one night last week because I thought Bill, who was driving, was drunk. I could smell alcohol as soon as he rolled down the window. But he blew below the limit. They were pretty nasty, but not nasty enough to arrest, unfortunately."

"Even Bill?"

"Yes, Sally, even Bill. I know he seems like he's the meek and mild one of the three, but I wouldn't trust him as far as I could throw him. I have a feeling he's the ringleader and gets the other two to do all his dirty work. But you know, other people are worse than the Grants. Tish, you should be very careful. Don't leave your car doors or your house doors unlocked even, especially, when you're home. For a small place, Setback has more than its share of shady characters."

Delmont was biting hard on the inside of her lip. She didn't like to have to listen even to the mention of Bill Grant's name, much less anything else about him or the rest of his family. Perhaps she would tell Terry Ross what he tried to pull with her.

"I'll be careful, Terry, don't worry. After all, I grew up in Chicago."

He gave her a warm smile. "So, you did."

As she paid the bill, she saw Sally and Terry Ross standing very close together just inside the restaurant door. Well, it had been worthwhile to be subjected to the local thugs and mediocre Chinese food just to see that. She hoped Sally would be married and in another part of Canada or wherever before she realized what had happened to her.

Tish brought Sally home to get her car after they left the restaurant. She liked having her car with her in case her mother called. Never knowing when she'd get a call in case Bette wasn't sleeping well.

The fire was crackling hot; the drinks were a cool counterpoint. The conversation was desultory, the result of full stomachs, alcohol, and heat.

Terry Ross suddenly got up and stretched, "I love this house and I love the company, but I have to go home and let Rex out."

For once, Sally was drained of colour. "Rex?"

"My golden retriever. He needs to go out right about now. But I can come back for a coffee later if you girls want me to."

Delmont saw her chance. "Well, that's a coincidence. I was meaning to call Jen over the weekend, to see how Bella's doing. Jen's my sister and Bella's my miniature dachshund. If I'm lucky, she'll bark into the phone when she holds it to her ear and I say "Hi, Bella!" Sally, why don't you go with Terry while he lets his dog out, and I'll call Jen, and I'll see you guys afterwards."

Sally looked down at her lap. Terry looked at Delmont and she gazed meaningfully at him. Tried some telepathy, although she didn't believe in it. *C'mon, Terry, take that girl home with you and keep her there.*

"Do you want to come with me, Sally? I'd certainly like the company." Terry sounded a bit too hearty, but it was probably just nerves.

Sally jumped up like a scalded cat. "Oh, sure, Terry. I love dogs."

After they left, Delmont went up to change into sweatpants and an old sweater. Because there was no way the two of them were coming back, she'd stake a sizeable amount of cold cash on that. She would settle down in front of the TV, the one she'd just gotten that week. There was no cable, but Canada had a national public broadcaster which wasn't bad. Tonight, they were running a Vietnam war documentary, which sounded intriguing. But then, anything was preferable to watching Sally make cow eyes at Terry Ross. Delmont was tired, from her trip and her "date" with Terry and Sally. Solitude never beckoned so sweetly.

Someone started pounding on the front door. Her heart started to pound as well: which one of the local creeps was trying to make her life more difficult than it needed to be? But then she heard Sally shouting her name. A strong gust of very cold wind hit her in the face.

Terry and Sally were standing on the steps; she looked scared, and he looked angry.

"Come in. What's up?"

"Someone slashed my tires. Every single one of them."

"Jesus on the barbeque. But I didn't hear anyone drive up."

"No. Whoever did it was no fool; they probably parked down the road and walked up. Gutsy fucker, sorry, I could've walked out of your house at any time and caught them."

Delmont got coffee for the three of them, and they sat at the kitchen table.

"So, Terry, do you have any idea who might have done it?"

Ross had assumed a sardonic smile. "Gee, where would I start. I'm not exactly the most loved person in Setback."

"But for someone to cut your tires, that's kind of juvenile."

"Police officers are always victims of vandalism and threats; it comes with the job. And there were several candidates at the restaurant tonight."

"Do you mean Rock McGee and the Grant brothers, Terry?" Sally's face was a combination of worry and disappointment. Delmont felt pity for her and her ruined night. Perhaps it could be salvaged, however.

"Terry, I'm sorry this had to happen at my house. Especially in the middle of such a pleasant evening."

"I'll have to get four new tires tomorrow. The cheapest ones they have in case someone has decided they are going to make slashing my tires a habit."

"I don't believe the garage is open on Sunday, Terry. They

only pump gas on Sundays." Sally's face had brightened up a bit.

"I'll get one of the boys who works at the garage to come by, pay him extra if I have to."

When they had gone – she told herself it was time to get a deadbolt on both doors.

Chapter 13

Delmont slept late. When she got up, the first thing
she did was look out of the bedroom window. Good, Terry
Ross's vehicle was gone, he must have gotten someone from
the garage to get it for him. And then she heard the sound of a
car engine. She hoped it wasn't Sally, coming to tell her all
about last night with Terry Ross. Well, she'd have to hear it
sometime, but she had hoped today wouldn't be the day. She
needed at least one day alone before she had to go back to
work, to run and think, catch up on some research, call a few
friends. But the vehicle coming in the drive wasn't Sally's. It
was her brother Rick's. Worse again.

She put on some clothes and went to see what he wanted.
When she opened the door, she saw Rick tossing firewood into
the barn.

"Rick, hey. What are you doing here? I didn't ask you for

firewood. I've got enough firewood to get into the firewood business. You need to put all that back in your truck. Besides, it's Sunday."

Rick spat on the ground. "Had nothin' better to do. I suppose in Chicargo you got to make an appointment to drop in on your neighbours, but we don't do that in Setback. And so, what if it's Sunday. I didn't figure you'd be in church."

Delmont tried to make her voice patient but could tell she wasn't having much success. "Look. I don't need any wood. I'm not paying for it. And, for the record, I don't think that's why you're really here, is it?"

Rick grinned. "I heard you were a smart girl. No, it isn't. Ask me in for a beer and I might tell you why I showed up here. Keep the fuckin' wood; it grows on trees, don't it?"

His guffaw was not as unpleasant as the word that described that kind of laugh. "Come in, then. But I don't have any beer. It's coffee, tea or water." would you like arsenic with that?

This was the second time she had been in close proximity to Sally's brother, and there was something about him that was nagging at her. Something that she felt she should have already picked up on. Intuition had been more useful to her professionally than her handful of university degrees.

Delmont could smell booze on him as soon as he had walked in. "I heard there was some action on the go out this way last night."

"Action? What kind of action?"

"Rumour goin' around town about a fella gettin' his tires slashed in your driveway last night."

She looked at him, wondering how much to tell him. "Yeah, that happened. Terry Ross and Sally and I went to dinner at the Chinese restaurant and then we came back here for a drink. Someone slashed his tires while he was here."

He had an ugly grin on his face now. "Oh, that's interestin'. Which one of you is a copsucker?'

"A *what*?"

"We calls the young ones around here who fuck cops, copsuckers. I'll laugh if it's my sister. Goin' from the piece of shit she was with to a cop."

"Your sister loved that piece of shit."

"Rex was a fuckin' idiot, a dopehead. He never treated Sally or Bette good."

"Didn't you ever hear of not speaking ill of the dead, Rick?"

"Oh, yeah, I heard that. Most people always say good stuff about people after they die. I don't; if you're a prick when you're alive, you're still a prick when you're dead. A prick above the ground and a prick when you gets laid in the ground. A lot of pricks in on boot hill in this community. But I never came here to talk about that prick Rex, I come here to talk about that fuckin' cunt Terry Ross." The last came out in a high voice, almost a falsetto.

Delmont realized that the palms of her hands had broken out in a sweat. Rick was more inebriated than she first thought, and he was in one vile mood. She tugged at her instincts – what were they saying? Apparently to let him talk; the hands were just a symptom of superficial nervousness. Down deep, she wanted to keep him talking. The boy needed to talk, and Delmont was starting to know what it was she didn't know about him before. Poor, poor Rick.

"What about Terry. Seems like a nice guy to me. A very nice guy. The kind of guy your sister could have a good life with, perhaps."

Rick laughed like a hyena. "Nice? Oh yes, he's real nice." Rick flapped a limp wrist in the air, and then he shouted, "He's a nice fuckin' faggot is what he is! Ask me how I knows. Go on, ask me."

By now the boy's twisted face was inches from Delmont's. She didn't really need to ask him how he knew Terry Ross was gay. She already knew.

"How do you know?"

This time Rick's voice was barely above a whisper. "Because the goddamn filthy bastard sucked my cock one night, that's how I knows. I'll spare you the details. I was drunk and he give me a ride home so I wouldn't be up for impaired. He took fuckin' advantage of me. And it never stopped there."

By now he was crying, sagging in the chair like a sack of potatoes. She got up and put her arms around him, letting him get it all out. Then she led him to the couch and sat down beside him.

"How long have you known you were gay, Rick?"

He reacted much more violently than she had expected, lifting his arms as though he was about to smash her in the face. She drew back and put her arm up to shield herself. But he dropped his arm and started crying again, softly this time. Like an animal in a trap that had no hope left. After a few minutes, he stopped and wiped his sleeve across his streaming eyes and nose. And then he looked at her.

"I'm not gay, missus. I never was and I wouldn't have done what I did if it wasn't for that evil cunt. He's a devil in the flesh and the sooner he's out of Setback the better. What I'm worried about is Sally. She doesn't know what he is, and I can't tell her, for obvious reasons. And the dirty bastard is only hangin' around her to get back at me for finally tellin' him to fuck off. He's playin' with her to spite me, I'll put a face on him with a baseball bat that a mother couldn't love, I will if he don't leave her alone. He wonders why no one doesn't like him. Well, it's because he's a fuckin' faggot, isn't it? A fuckin' smarmy know-it-all faggot from up along. We don't like those kinds around here"

Delmont's heart felt like it was two sizes too big for her chest. No, they didn't like "faggots" in Setback. And poor Rick was one. And so, he had to hate Terry Ross as much as he hated himself. More, in fact. She thought about talking to Ross about the situation. But no. Her intuition told her that Rick was no threat to Ross. He just needed counselling, and possibly medication. Why hadn't she picked up on the fact that Ross was gay? Well, not all gay men were obvious. She'd once dated one for three months without realizing he was never going to sleep with her. She'd thought he was just shy. Poor Rick, poor Sally.

"Rick don't worry about Sally. She has a little crush on him, that's all. She told me she could never see herself leaving Setback with Bette. She said it's the best place in the world to bring up a kid. And you know how attached she is to you and your parents."

"I suppose." Rick's face brightened up, but then clouded over again. "Listen, you won't say nothin' about any of this to no one, right? Because I'll know where it comes from. And if you thinks you can destroy my life, you better think again."

"Rick, I'm a professional counsellor. I am not allowed to say anything to anyone, including authorities such as the police, about what is said to me in confidence by a patient, unless it involves a serious crime and or criminal activity. Technically, you are not my patient, but as far as I'm concerned, as of this morning, we do have that relationship – psychologist and patient."

Rick stood up abruptly. And then he leaned down and kissed her hard on the cheek. "Thanks, Doc. I got to go now. You keep that firewood, okay?"

Chapter 14

WHEN DELMONT ARRIVED AT THE TOWN HALL ON MONDAY morning, Sally wasn't in her office. She hoped the girl had not come to grief over the weekend with Terry Ross. Maybe Ross wasn't gay, but bisexual. Either way, she would have to figure out something; Sally must be pried from the handsome but unsuitable RCMP officer.

Two hours later, she heard Sally's door open and close. Delmont took her cup of coffee and went to investigate. She knocked on the door first, just in case.

"Come in."

"Sally, hey. You're in late this morning." Late and with the glummest face, she had ever seen on a human being. Sally looked like Bella when she knew Delmont was leaving the apartment without her.

"Bette had a Doctor's appointment for a vaccination."

Delmont sat down on the ancient wooden office chair that looked like it had come over on the *Mayflower*. If the *Mayflower* had ever been in these waters. She thought she'd read that it had stopped in Renews on the Southern Shore for supplies. Even the sturdy Puritans must have been dismayed by the landscape, or lack of it, rather. A cold, barren sameness punctuated by trees.

"So, how was your weekend." Delmont resolved to tread carefully.

"Okay."

"Okay, was it?" Then why do you have tears in your eyes, poor child?

"No. It was awful." The tears came brimming over, and Sally grabbed a tissue out of the box on her desk.

"Want to talk about it? If you don't, that's okay."

"I guess. I'm upset about Terry, but you probably know that."

"I figured. What happened?"

"Nothin'. And that's the problem. We had such a good time at your place, and when I drove him home and he asked me in, I thought things were goin' to get even better. And for a while they did. We talked and talked – he wanted to know everythin' about me and my family – even asked me a bunch of questions about Rick. I got the impression he likes him, maybe even thinks Rick got potential if he'd straighten up. And then he put his arms around me, and – well – I didn't feel nothin'. I thought I'd be the happiest girl in Setback if he ever did that, but I wasn't. And then he kissed me, and that was worse – I felt – what's the word –"

"Repelled?"

"Yes, that's the word, all right. Like he was some kind of negative force. What do you suppose went wrong? I had such a thing for him, Tish."

"Well, Sally, speaking as a professional who's dealt with a lot of relationship problems, I can think of one or two things it might be. He might be in a serious relationship back home and got cold feet with you at the last minute, and that's what you were feeling off him. Or you two just might not be sexually compatible. It happens. Either way, he's a good guy, just not the right one for you."

"But don't you think it might be something else?"

"Like what?"

"That I'm not good enough for him, and he realized it?"

Delmont laughed before she could stop herself. Oh, Sally, it's not that you're not good enough, it's just that you don't have a penis like your brother. She willed her face into solemnity. "No, Sally, that's not an option. No man in the world could resist you unless there was something else going on. Another relationship is my strong professional hunch."

Sally looked like some of the weight of the world had been taken from her shoulders. She sighed. "Oh well. It was nice while it lasted. The fantasy, I mean."

"Never mind, girl, Prince Charming is out there

somewhere. Not to change the subject, but I guess I am: do you know the Nagle brothers?"

"Yes, but not well. Bill and Harry Nagle are from the north side of the harbour; they're weird. And antisocial. They live opposite your house across the harbour. Got a bunch of different kinds of farm animals."

"Just my luck. Two more weirdos around my place. The landlord is sending them over to do some repairs on the house and put deadbolts on my doors. I'm starting to feel like I live next to an asylum." At least this made Sally laugh. Cheer up my girl – you don't know how lucky you are to be rid of Terry Ross.

On Saturday morning, just as Delmont had closed the front door after getting back from a run, someone knocked on it. She opened it; on the other side were two older bearded men dressed in clothing that looked thirty years old and had not seen a washing machine since they were bought. The larger of the two men said, in a gruff voice, "We're here to fix your house. What's wrong with it?"

Well, no beating around the bush with these Nagle brothers. "The back door is hard to close, and some of the windows are drafty. I also need the chimney checked to see if it needs cleaning. And the landlord left two deadbolts here that I need installed."

The two men grunted in unison and pushed by her. Sally hadn't been kidding about strange.

The phone rang. It was Sally, and she was upset. Her voice was at least two octaves higher than normal. "Tish, oh my God, somethin' really bad has happened to Terry. There was a fight at Longview last night, and the RCMP were called to attend, and Terry went there by himself. Stupid, stupid, but he was the only officer on duty. Rock was into it with two men from St. John's who were out here moose huntin'." Her voice cracked. "Rock turned on Terry, he beat him up and beat him bad. They took him by ambulance to the hospital in Gander. They say his face was all cut up and some of his teeth knocked out and he probably got a few broken ribs."

"Oh crap, Sally. Are you all right?"

"I'll live, but poor Terry, it's a mortal sin. Apparently, three Mounties came in from Gander a few hours later and arrested Rock at his house. He's been charged with assaultin' a peace officer and resistin' arrest. He never went quietly because he's a fuckin' madman."

Sally, swearing? She must be really upset. But so was Delmont. Setback was starting to erode her.

"Sally, do you think we should go to the hospital in Gander? I mean, Terry doesn't have any family or friends here. Maybe he'd like some visitors." Delmont regretted the words as soon as they were out of her mouth. She didn't want anything more to do with Terry Ross, even if he had been badly injured. Too late now. She wondered if he was still pretty with missing teeth.

"Good idea," said Sally. "I'll call the hospital and ask what his status is. I'll call you back as soon as I find out."

"Okay."

The phone rang again fifteen minutes later. "I spoke to the hospital, Tish. They're lettin' him go tomorrow. It's not as bad as I heard. One broken tooth, eight stitches in his face, and two bruised ribs, one on either side. They are keepin' him overnight as a precaution, he may be concussed."

"Why do you think Rock beat Terry Ross so badly? I mean, you told me that the Mounties go to Longview half a dozen times a year to break up fights. They usually help Rock break up fights."

"Well, to tell you the truth, Tish, the only thing I can think of is that Rock has a bit of a thing for you – I could see that the night he drove us home from Longview, and you told me he tried to pick you up on the road one day. And he saw you with Terry and me at Hong's that night. I wouldn't be at all surprised if that's at the bottom of it all."

Delmont couldn't believe her ears. "Sally, that can't be right. I mean, if it is, he's a psychopath." Which wouldn't come as a total surprise to her.

"What's that?"

"Someone with such a severe mental illness that he or she is completely unable to relate to other people, emotionally.

They're egotistic and extremely violent. No conscience. Unless he's one of those, there must be more to this story."

"I told you he was nuts, didn't I? But you're right; I'm not sure he's that nuts. Maybe there is somethin' else goin' on. Tish, could you come over and maybe watch a movie with me tonight? I'd be glad to have some company. I picked up a copy of a movie called *Basic Instinct* at the convenience store earlier. It's supposed to be good."

Delmont burst out laughing. "Oh, Sally!"

"What?"

"I saw it last year when it came out. It's about a psychopath. A woman."

"No way."

"Yup. I'll pick up another movie on the way over?"

When she arrived at Sally's with a copy of *Benny and Joon,* Rick's truck was parked in the driveway. Damn, damn, damn. Oh well, perhaps he wouldn't mind running into her here. She'd mind, though. She'd had enough drama for one day.

As she stepped out of the car, she saw Rick coming out of the side door to Sally's house. He waved when he saw her and kept going, staggering slightly. Good. She hoped he wouldn't come back this evening, but also that he'd make it home safely. At least Terry Ross wouldn't be around to try to pick him up.

She knocked on the door and heard Sally say, "Come in,

it's not locked. You don't need to knock on doors in Setback, you just walk in."

Delmont grimaced. Her door was definitely a Chicago door, you had to knock. And then verbally identify yourself. "Hi, Sally, how are you feeling?"

"Okay, I guess. Did you see Rick? He just left."

"I saw him on the way in. He appeared to have a buzz on."

"Since the fishery collapsed, he's drinkin' most days."

The boy had more problems than his loss of livelihood, but she wasn't about to tell Sally that. "That's too bad. But it happens all over the world, you know. Traditional industries collapse, people react badly, but in time they adjust. People survive – it's human nature. Rick's strong; he'll come around eventually. He's bright, too – maybe you could talk him into going to the city and taking a trade." And then he could go to the gay bars and, with any luck, meet some nice men.

Sally looked doubtful. "Oh, Rick could do a trade, all right – he'd ace her. Smart as a whip when he puts his mind to somethin'. But I'd hate to see him go to St. John's, I would. Me and Bette thinks the world of him. And so do Mom and Dad, of course."

"St. John's isn't that far away, Sally. And he wouldn't be gone forever. You went away yourself and survived. If he stays here and the fishery doesn't recover, I don't think he'll do too well, do you?" He needs to go forever, Delmont thought. He might have half a chance of being happy then.

"Oh, Tish, don't say that about the fishery never comin'

back – that doesn't bear thinkin' about. Anyway, do you want anythin' to drink?"

"A cup of coffee will do. I like your house, by the way. It's cozy." Just slightly better than tacky cozy, but it had charm. Sally's sweet energy had infused the conventional furniture and somewhat tawdry decor.

"Thanks. I guess you must miss your place in Chicago."

"I do. Not that I'm there much, but it's a refuge when I need one."

"I can't imagine livin' in an apartment. What's your landlord like?"

"I don't have a landlord. I bought the apartment. People do buy flats, as they call them in Europe. In parts of Europe, owning a house is rare."

"Imagine. Have you ever been to Europe?"

"Yes, several times. You should go – it's beautiful. Old and beautiful."

"Some of the buildin's around here are a couple of hundred years old. The house you live in is pretty old too."

"In Europe, a couple of hundred years is nothing. I went to a seminar at Oxford University in England once: it's about a thousand years old."

"A thousand years? I didn't think they had universities back then. Or anythin' much."

"Well, a thousand years ago in Newfoundland, there was nothing much. The land and the sea, and a handful of Vikings at one point. And some natives."

"And now there's me and you – and a university. Memorial in St. John's."

"Yes, I've been there. I was surprised, actually, at how big it is. And how sophisticated. Where's Bette, Sally? Asleep?"

"No, I dropped her at Moms. She's been sleepin' lightly these past few weeks – I was afraid we'd wake her up."

"That's too bad. For me, I mean. I was looking forward to meeting her."

"Do you want to take a run over to my parents? They're dyin' to meet you, after everythin' I've been tellin' them. It's okay if you don't"

Delmont saw the look and Sally's face and knew she'd be disappointed if the answer was no. And she wouldn't mind, really. Johnny Depp could wait.

A tiny, waifish blond child threw herself at Sally the moment she and Delmont were over Sally's parents' threshold. Delmont was reminded of Bella, who always managed to be at the apartment door even before she put the key in the lock. Kids and dogs must have the same animal radar.

"Bette, look who's here! This is Tish, remember I told you about her? The new woman where I works?"

The child remained hanging onto her mother, but she turned her head and shot Tish a shy grin. And then she buried her face in her mother's coat as if she'd run out of bravery. The cockles of Delmont's heart warmed; perhaps she should get herself one of those? But no – the whim faded as quickly as it had appeared, and her cockles went back to their natural tepid state. Too much personal responsibility, and, besides, Bella would be jealous.

"Come into the livin' room and meet my parents, Tish." Sally led the way, her daughter clinging to her hand.

Sally's parents were sitting on the couch watching TV. Her mother was an older copy of the girl, worn around the edges, she was attractive for her age. Delmont noted her listlessness and general air of defeat and wasn't surprised. Sally would look that way too if she stayed in Setback and married here. The father, on the other hand, seemed vital and animated. He jumped up and greeted them in a voice that would carry in a storm.

"Come in, come in, come in! Sally is always talkin' about you – good things, mind you. So, you've come all the way from up in Chicargo, have you? Just to help us poor folks out now that they took the fishery on us. Well, I for one don't believe it's the end of the line for the cod; they've been here for dog's years, and we been fishin' them for five hundred years. They'll bounce back, and then I'll be out chasin' them again, I will so. Betty, get Dr. Delmont a cup of tea and some of them biscuits you made earlier."

This last was a barked order. Sally's mother rose slowly to her feet and went towards the kitchen. Delmont mentally entertained the thought of picking up the fireplace poker and hitting Sally's father over the head with it. No man had ever spoken to her like that, nor ever would. If he knew what was good for him.

"If you wants, you can both have a plate of supper – we had leftover Jiggs' dinner, and the wife can fry you up some if you wants it."

"No, that's fine, Mr. Osmond –"

"Jack."

"Jack. I had dinner before I went to Sally's." Thank God. The thought of fried – in lard, probably – cured meat and greasy cabbage made Delmont's stomach do a slight flip.

"And I ate before Tish came to the house, Dad."

The four of them sat and talked for an hour over the best cup of tea Delmont had ever had, not to mention the best raisin biscuits. Sally's father monopolized the conversation with a lecture on the history of the fishery; he was trying to impress Delmont, she knew. But she was not impressed, just bored. She'd already read all the fishery in preparation for her stint in Setback.

Finally, Sally told her parents that she and Delmont were going back to her house to watch a movie. At this point, Delmont would have been happy to watch Sharon Stone boil that bunny.

"So, if you needs to know anythin' about the fishery, ducky, you can give me a call anytime." Jack Osmond was puffed up like a pigeon on the make. No, thanks, you pompous ass, Delmont said silently.

Sally's mother spoke up. Delmont was startled. The woman had barely uttered a word. "Dr. Delmont, do you suppose you could help Sally find a man while you're here? She doesn't seem to be too good at it herself."

Delmont repressed a smile. Why would she be any good at it? Her mother sure hadn't been. "I'll see what I can do, Mrs. Osmond – Betty."

"I suppose you're single yourself, are you? Or else you wouldn't be traipsin' around by yourself down here."

"Yes, I'm single." And so grateful to be, especially confronted by a marriage like yours.

"Hard to believe you two beautiful girls are single."

"Tish and me are picky, Mom."

"In my day, no one was picky. If a decent man showed an interest in you, you married him."

Was there bitterness in Betty's voice? Hard to tell, the woman likely wouldn't dare express herself further on the subject of marriage.

"Mom, you know times have changed."

"I guess they have." This time there was emotion in Betty's voice: sorrow. Whether for the changing times or for her inability to enjoy them, Delmont didn't know. But she bet it was the latter.

As they walked to the car, Delmont said, "Would you mind going for a little drive? There are lots of places in this town I haven't seen yet. I'd like to see where the Nagle brothers live. They did a great job on the repairs and installing the deadbolts. But they are two weird dudes."

Sally giggled. "I love it when you talks American."

In a few minutes, Delmont and Sally arrived at the dilapidated house on the north shore of the harbour. Well, the Nagles might be good at house repairs, but they sure didn't look after their own. The roof looked as if it were ready to blow off in the next soft breeze. A dog of an indeterminate breed was tied beside the front door, curled in a ball, trying to keep warm on this bitter night. If Delmont hadn't been sure there was no local humane society, she would have gone home and called them. She shuddered to think what condition the other animals they owned were in.

"Tish, there's a really good band playin' tonight at Longview. A rock-and-roll band. Want to stop in for a drink? I mean, we can go back and watch the movie if you rather."

Delmont did not want to go back to Longview for any reason. But she'd humour Sally. The girl didn't have much of a life, and if it cheered her up to hang out in that swamp for an hour or two, well, Delmont could take it.

"Sure, if you want."

"I don't want to take the car, though. We're right by Mom and Dad's; how about I get him to drive us?"

"He won't mind?"

"No, they got me spoiled. When Rex passed, Mom and Dad couldn't do enough for Bette and me. They hated to see me in pain. Poor old Rex." Sally's mouth emitted a small gust of wind. "But enough about Rex, that'll only spoil our night."

Jack Osmond didn't seem to mind driving the girls to the club. Delmont thought about what her mother would have said should she ever have asked for a ride to a nightclub. "What's wrong – are there no taxis left in Chicago?" Sally kissed her father before she got out of the car. Sally looked hopefully at Tish, but she pretended she hadn't seen.

The club was packed. Delmont was surprised, but not too surprised. Alcohol was a major problem in Setback, and the closure of the fishery had exacerbated it. This crowded bar was a case in point. She should talk to the Mounties; perhaps they could step up drunk-driving patrols. Not everyone's father was willing to drive them to the bar.

Delmont and Sally got drinks at the bar – a soda and lemon for Delmont, a rum and Coke for Sally – and they found a table; Delmont insisted it be near the door. She sat down in the chair that was closest to the wall and looked around. The bouncer, Rock McGee was there, of course, she'd had to walk past him on the way in. He'd looked like he was in a foul mood, and hadn't said a word to her, or even to Sally, who'd greeted him with a rather large, if nervous, "Hi!" The Grant brothers were there, and so was Rick, hanging off the end of the bar with his friend Dave. Sally noticed Delmont looking at Rick and wrinkled up her nose.

"I hates drunk Rick as much as I loves sober Rick. He's nasty and rude to me and Mom and Dad and everyone else. If anyone should never drink, it's him."

Delmont agreed with that. On top of his homosexuality, he was probably a depressive. Homosexuals were more at risk of depression, bipolar disorder, and substance abuse than straight people. Delmont felt sorry for them; they already had enough to cope within a world that was hostile to deviations from the norm. But, of course, some of their mental health problems were related to the hostility they endured. One of Delmont's closest friends was gay. She wished he was here right now. She could use one of his special cocktails, and his comforting sense of humour. Well, maybe not here, not at Longview, he'd have his head beaten in before you could say Liberace.

Sally was up dancing in no time. No one asked Delmont to dance, which was fine by her. She guessed they still thought she was a lesbian, which was fine by her also. The Grant brothers kept staring at Sally and her with nasty looks on their faces, but that was just what they did, the Grant brothers. Sat around looking mean.

The next time Sally danced, she brought the guy back to their table.

"Tish, this is Jimmy Parsons, the local fire captain. He's goin' to drive us back to my house right now – isn't that nice of him?"

Delmont thought it was downright swell. She couldn't wait to get home. And Parsons looked like a nice chap, a few years older than Sally, short and stocky, honest face, didn't seem to be drunk. Well, there had to be one piece of gold among all the tin.

On their way through the town, Sally spotted Terry Ross. He had a car pulled over and was standing talking to the driver.

"Jimmy, stop the car. I want to say hi to Terry and see how he's doin'. What a mess that crazy Rock made of him."

Parsons kept driving. "Not a chance. I'm not pullin' over for that prick – correction, he's two pricks."

"Jimmy! That's a terrible thing to say, especially comin' from a fire captain. You guys usually have a good workin' relationship with the Mounties. Anyway, Tish and I like him."

"Well, you two are in the minority. Worst cop we've ever had here, and we've had a few dandies. Walks around with his chest stuck out like he owns the place. Rock never beat him hard enough."

Driving home later that night, Delmont slightly changed her opinion of the fire captain. He wasn't as harmless as he'd seemed, but compared to the other local men she'd met, he was definitely a cut above. Sally wouldn't mind some roughness; God knows, she was used to a lot worse.

Chapter 15

DELMONT HAD AWAKENED TO WHAT SOUNDED LIKE SPRING: THE drip of melting water from her eavestroughs. This time of year, late February, was famous for its false springs, she'd heard the locals say. Well, even if it lasted for a few days, it was as welcome as the real spring. She decided to go for a run in the newly soft air. But just as she was pulling on her sweatpants, there was a knock on the door. Oh, Jesus in short pants, what now? Had the Nagle brothers forgotten their hammer?

When she opened the door, she was greeted by Sally's distraught face.

"Oh, Tish, I got terrible news. More terrible news about Terry – he's missin'!"

"Missing?"

"Yeah, I was out with Bette goin' down to the takeout to

get some wings and fries for our lunch when I saw three
RCMP cruisers drivin' by, and we only got two at the
detachment. And Terry wasn't drivin' neither of them. And
when I passed the fire hall, the doors were open. So, I figured
there was a fire somewhere. But when I got to the takeout, the
girls behind the counter asked me if I'd heard the news – they
were right wild with it. No, I said, what news? And they said
Terry Ross is missin' – never contacted the detachment since
three this mornin'. They said Setback is crawlin' with cops.
Apparently, there's even some here from St. John's. Half the
harbour is searchin' for him. There's even a helicopter here
from Gander, and another one on the way from St. John's. And
the girls were sayin' how everybody hates Terry. I don't know
how they could!"

The last sentence came out in a wail; Delmont grabbed the
Kleenex box and pushed it across the table.

"Calm down, Sally. We saw him on the way home,
remember? I'm sure Terry's fine, and they'll find him soon."
She didn't, of course, think either of these things, but there
was no sense in adding to Sally's misery. Setback had a black
underbelly; only God knew where Terry Ross was, or in what
kind of shape.

Sally's wails had slowed to sniffles. "Yes, I remember
seein' him. Jimmy said . . . you know what Jimmy said. And
he's normally so quiet and nice – everyone respects Jimmy
Parsons. So why do they all hate Terry? I know Jimmy said
it's because he thinks too much of himself – which he don't,

they just says that because they knows he *is* better than most of them, and it makes them feel small."

Good for you, Sally. That's the gist of it, but there's also his questionable sexuality, which they might be picking up on as well. What else needed to be factored in.

"I just hope he never came upon somethin' untoward, like the Grants poachin' big game. Because I wouldn't doubt, they'd just as soon kill him and hope to get away with it than face a judge."

"That's pretty extreme, Sally." And yet, Delmont had a gut feeling that the girl wasn't indulging in the dramatic excess that so many inhabitants of Setback enjoyed. If they'd only read some good fiction, they'd probably tone it down a bit. She'd come across a theory that said all those witches were burned at the stake because hundreds of years ago, there was no other entertainment. When the novel was invented, we became more civilized.

"I hate to say it, Tish, but there are a few in this town who are capable of murder. Remember the story I told you about Walter Grant killin' Gerry Lyver? Well, I wouldn't be shocked if one of the Grants has blood on their hands. And Rock hasn't been in court yet on his charges for beatin' up Terry. Poor Terry. He was so sweet when we went out to dinner that night. I pray he's all right. Maybe he ran the cruiser over an embankment somewhere and he's trapped. Maybe his radio got busted and he couldn't radio the detachment. Maybe he's unconscious or worse. Could you turn on the radio, Tish, and see if there's any news?"

Delmont got up and turned on the radio, switching the dial from CBC to the local Gander station, CKGA. She and Sally sat down on the couch beside the table on which the radio stood, and Sally put her head on Delmont's shoulder. Tears intermittently streaked her cheeks. After several songs had played, the news came on. The first story was about Terry Ross's disappearance. The announcer related the circumstances of his disappearance and then went on to say that a manhunt was ongoing in the Setback area, involving officers from Gander and St. John's, Search and Rescue, volunteer fire department members from the community, and dozens of community members from Setback.

"Well, that didn't tell us anything we didn't already know." Delmont switched off the radio – she couldn't stand one more seventies disco track – and got up to put on more coffee.

"Tish, I'm goin' to call Dad. If anyone has heard anythin', it will be him."

"Great idea, Sally." Delmont went upstairs to put on a T-shirt that didn't have tears on it and to make a few phone calls herself. To the outside world, that didn't even know where Setback was. It would be good to hear her sister's voice right now.

When Delmont came back downstairs, Sally was sitting by the phone, looking dejected. She tried to smile at Delmont and failed.

"What's up, Sally, what did you hear?"

"Well, Tish, Dad didn't know anythin' more than we do. I asked him if Rick was home, he might have heard somethin' – he's worse than a woman for rumours. But Dad said Rick never came home until four in the mornin', and he was up again at nine and gone off on his trike. Which is strange because he never gets up early these days. I told him I'd be over around suppertime to pick up Bette and to call me if he heard anythin'."

Sally didn't seem to be in a hurry to leave. Delmont suspected that the girl wanted her company until the suspense was over, one way or another. Christ on a three-wheeler – she needed to be alone, and she needed to get some work done. But it was just one day out of her life, after all.

"Sally, I'll make some sandwiches, you just sit there and relax."

Sally looked relieved. "I'm goin' to call the mayor. He probably knows somethin'."

When Delmont got back with the plate of sandwiches and coffee, Sally still looked glum. Either she'd heard something bad from the mayor, or she'd heard nothing.

"So, Sally, anything to report?"

"No, nothin'. He called an emergency meetin' at the fire hall this mornin' – the RCMP and Search and Rescue asked him to, they were there also. Lots of people showed up to volunteer to look for Terry. They got groups of two and three men to search specific areas. But no one has found anythin' yet, neither Terry nor his cruiser. And they haven't got any leads. If they don't find him by dark, they're goin' to expand the search tomorrow to other communities around here, east, and west. They're all goin' to meet again tomorrow mornin' at seven. He's expectin' hundreds to come, from Black Tree and even way over to Pine Stock. They have two helicopters in the air now, and they'll be puttin' another one on at daybreak, and an RCMP plane, if they don't find him. He said he'd call me the minute he heard anythin'. I'm pretty sure he knows I liked Terry, Tish."

Delmont could sense more tears – that didn't take a giant leap of the imagination – and she quickly tried to put a stop to them. "Sally, why don't we go for a drive and then pick Bette up, and you two can drop me back here."

A wan smile, but no tears.

"Okay, Tish. That should take my mind off it a bit."

They drove around the harbour under a sky the colour of pewter. Winter had come back. The temperature was close to zero. Delmont tried not to think about what might be happening to Terry Ross if he was still alive. If he'd been badly hurt and was trapped inside his cruiser or crawling through the thick trees that bracketed barren Setback, he wouldn't last long in this weather.

They heard the big yellow helicopters before they saw them. Two big airborne beasts, like dragons, on either side of the harbour, scanning the coast with floodlights. Darkness was setting in.

"This is not lookin' good, Tish."

"Why not?" She knew damn well why not, but it was easier to listen to Sally talk than cry.

"Well, look at them – up there searchin' the coast. What if Terry went into the ocean and his cruiser is under the water with him in it?"

Oh, Lord. Apparently, the girl could talk *and* cry.

"Now, Sally, don't be pessimistic. And you'd better settle down before we get Bette, or you'll upset her."

"I'm sorry, Tish. But he wouldn't be the first person to go through a guardrail and into the water, more specifically the Atlantic Ocean."

"Sally, stop!" Crap! She hadn't meant to sound so harsh. She could feel the girl stiffen up beside her in the seat.

"I'm sorry. I'm only statin' a fact."

"No, you're not, you're jumping into a black hole feet first like a five-year-old, without considering me, or logic." Delmont had noticed the lack of emotional maturity in Setback. Sometimes it was attractive, sometimes – like now – really not.

Bette was at the window when they pulled into Sally's parents' driveway. The girl ran straight into her mother's arms like an arrow to a target as soon as they got in the door. Delmont wondered what kind of problems the child would have later in life, no one ever got out of childhood completely intact, after all. She knew what it was like not to have a father. But, like Bette, she also knew what it was like to have a loving mother. And Bette had Newfoundland grandparents, also a plus, at least in this culture.

Sally's father was sitting at the kitchen table, looking across the harbour through a pair of black binoculars. He was drinking a cup of tea and having a smoke.

"Hello, girls! Do ye want a cup of tea? Betty, get in here and get the girls a cup of tea. Oh, I forgot – your mother's gone next door for a cup of tea and a chat."

"That's all right, Dad, I'll get the tea." Sally filled the kettle and put it on the stove.

Delmont was amazed but not amused. Here was a grown man who was incapable of making a simple cup of tea. Men seem to be treated either like kings or small children in Setback, neither of which was good for them. Or for the women and children. But it was ever thus in rural communities. She suddenly had such a longing for home that she felt weak in the knees.

Sally's father noticed Tish's discomfort. He patted the kitchen chair beside him. "Come have a seat, my dear; you don't look so hot. It's all this racket about Terry, I suppose, and you and Sally knew him."

Sally brought tea and toast and homemade bakeapple jam and butter to the table. Delmont realized that all the fuss had made her hungry and accepted a large helping of everything.

"Dad, have you heard anythin' about Terry yet? What about Rick – did he hear anythin'?"

"No, my darlin', that's what I haven't. As for Rick, he

hasn't been home since nine this mornin'. That boy has gotten into bad ways since the fishery collapsed. Drinkin' all the time, hangin' out with hard cases. I hear he's tangled up with that McGee fella, the one from Longview. The bouncer. Everyone knows that's as mad as three waltzin' mice."

Delmont smiled. What a lovely turn of phrase. Much more pleasing to the ear than "fucking crazy."

Sally looked perturbed. "I didn't know that Dad. That Rick and Rock were friends."

"Well, I heard that a few weeks ago. I don't know if there's any truth to it. Usually, where there's smoke, there's fire."

They left an hour or so later, after another short lecture on the fishery. Delmont rather liked Sally's father, all the same. He was a kind man, if not a developed one. And that was the main thing, after all. Kindness. If only you could inject people with it.

When they reached the lane to Delmont's house, Bette leaned over the front seat and kissed Delmont on the ear, just the way Bella kissed her sometimes.

"Aw, Bette – you kiss even better than my dog."

Sally laughed and Bette giggled. Delmont started to get out of the car, but Sally reached out and held on to her arm.

"I don't feel good about this."

Oh, for the love of God, as the locals said. "Why?"

"Well, here's a run-through for you. Rock beat Terry up, the Grant brothers are poachin' everythin' that has four legs or swims and they're known for their bad tempers. Walter is dangerous, which most likely makes his brothers dangerous as well. There are drugs all over this town and all along the coast. What if Terry came upon a shipment of drugs, maybe comin' in somewhere by boat the other night, and he was killed before he could call it in? His body may never be found. It could be sittin' on the bottom of the ocean or a pond in the country somewhere, with a grapnel tied to it. He wouldn't be the first police officer to disappear and never be found."

"Sally, I think you must have swallowed that mystery novel you said you were reading. Stuff like that happens in Chicago, not in small rural places like Setback."

"Tish, the world is changin', and Newfoundland is changin' with it. Not only is weed and hash easy to get, but cocaine, acid, and even heroin are also easy to get these days. Rex had no trouble findin' all that stuff, and he didn't have to go all the way to St. John's or Gander to find it, either."

"Sally, go home and try to relax. This isn't doing you or Bette any good. Or Terry either."

Delmont got out of the car and walked towards the house. Sally had already turned around and was headed home. She was halfway to her doorstep when she saw a Search and Rescue van and two RCMP cruisers parked on the road a hundred feet from the white wooden cross. She shuddered, whether, from the easterly wind or the idea of evil having been done so close to her house, she couldn't tell.

She decided to call Sally.

"Sally, it's Tish. There's a Search and Rescue van and two RCMP vehicles parked by the cross on my road."

"Well, somethin's up, I saw them, after droppin' you off - why else would they be there? I bet they're checkin' that spot because it's where Walter Grant tried to hide Lyver's body and car after he murdered him. It's steep and goes a fair ways down. I'm goin' to call Dad again."

Sally called Delmont an hour later, just as she was deep in a paper about female genital mutilation. She wasn't too upset about being disturbed.

"Sally, hi – any news?"

"Not really. After I got Bette bathed and in bed and read a story to her – she's just wild about *The Three Little Pigs* - I phoned Dad. The only thing he could tell me is that he thought the search would be delayed in the mornin' because the weather forecast is callin' for strong northerly winds and snow overnight and into mid-day. He said they wouldn't put choppers in the air with high winds forecasted. He also told me that when Walter Grant killed Gerry Lyver, they were four or five days lookin' for Gerry's body before they found it. I was too young when that happened, don't remember a thing about it. And Rick hasn't shown up yet – out drunk somewhere, I guess. Anyway, see you at work in the mornin'."

Poor Rick. Probably at Longview drowning his ambivalent feelings about Terry Ross. Delmont wished she could do something for the boy, but unless he came to see her professionally, there wasn't much she could do. Maybe get in touch with his GP and talk to him or her about the bad shape Rick was in. Because Rick certainly had never had that conversation with his Doctor. Maybe the GP could talk him into a course of antidepressants. Rick was heading for cirrhosis down the road. Something nasty, anyway. Delmont suddenly felt as though someone had walked over her grave.

Chapter 16

THE TEMPERATURE HAD DROPPED HARD OVERNIGHT, AND A northeast gale with snow in its fist was pummeling Setback. Delmont lit the fire as soon as she got up. She was going to call Sally and tell her that she would be working at home today, and then call her clients to reschedule. They would be reluctant to go out in this, just as reluctant as she was. The house was drafty, but she didn't mind. She liked houses that breathed.

The phone rang; doubtless, it was Sally, with or without some news. She needed another phone jack, upstairs. She had a habit of forgetting the cordless phone. The old stairs were uncarpeted and slippery, not safe for running up and down. She quickly slid into her sneakers with the good treads and got to the phone after it had rung about ten times. It was either

Sally or a work emergency. Not that there'd been many of those.

"Tish, hi, guess what? We don't have to go to work today. I was just talkin' to Mayor White, they have the town hall all set up as a command post for the search. He said there was still nothin' to report, except that the search was held off until the weather got better. I told him I'd go in if he needed me. I hate to think of Terry out there somewhere, but it's nice to have a day off when you aren't expectin' it. Want to come to hang out?"

"Sally, I'd love to, but I have so much work piled up. I really have to get at it. And I need to be alone, girl. I need to recharge."

"But, Tish, how can you do any work if you're not at work?"

"I have reports to write, research to do – and a paper for a journal I've been working on for six months to finish."

"Oh."

The disappointment in Sally's voice was palpable; Delmont knew the girl hadn't really understood what Delmont was talking about, had likely thought she was making stuff up to avoid seeing her. Oh well, one more day with Sally wouldn't kill her – would it? Delmont didn't have a high boredom threshold.

"Never mind, Sally. I'll be over in a couple of hours if that's okay with you? If my road gets ploughed. I'll call you if I can't make it."

"Sure, Tish, that would be great."

As she was hanging up the phone, Delmont heard the snowplow approaching and resigned herself to her fate.

The snow was still falling, but it was light, it didn't take Delmont much time to clear off her car. When she passed the white cross, indistinct against the snow and half-buried in it, there were no vehicles or vehicle tracks.

Sally's parents were at their daughter's house when Delmont arrived. They all looked as solemn as a small parliament of owls, and Delmont almost grinned but didn't. Such solemnity boded ill.

"So, Sally, what's the news?"

"Rick didn't come home last night. The only time he doesn't sleep home is when he's at his cabin in over the ridge."

"Does it have a heating system?" Delmont shivered inwardly at the idea of being in an unheated shelter in this weather. And why would anyone have a cabin who lived in Setback? When she was a child, her mother would sometimes rent a cottage in the country in the summers, just so they could get away from the city for a while. All you got away from in a cabin in the woods near Setback was – what?

"Of course, it does – a woodstove, like all the cabins."

"Well, maybe he went there with some friends yesterday and stayed overnight, and he's still there because of the weather."

"That makes sense," said Sally's mother. "I never factored in the weather."

"Mom, I wouldn't worry about Rick. He's rough and tough, he'll be fine, I'm sure."

Sally's father spoke next. "I heard a rumour this mornin'. Apparently, Wildlife and the RCMP were only days away from bustin' the Grant boys for poachin'. Apparently, they've been at it all fall. After killin' dozens of moose and caribou."

"I know, Dad. I heard that one myself,"

"Where did you hear it to?"

"I can't remember. Probably at work. You know there are dozens of people comin' and goin' at the town hall every day. One of them likely told me. It's hard to keep track of all the gossip in this town."

"I wouldn't want to be huntin' down them Grants. They're dangerous men, and not to be messed with. Especially when they're drinkin'. Bill, he's the worst one of the three. He's sly, always gettin' them other two dimwits to do his dirty work. Everyone says he's a fine fella because Bill is the only one with a woman. The other two can't keep a woman or a job. In and out of court every other month on some stupid charge."

"Dad, you and Mom want to stay for lunch with me and Tish?"

"No thank you, darlin' – we got to pick up a few groceries and get home out of it. Nice seein' you again, Tish. Bet you don't have days like this down south in Chicargo."

"Not exactly." Almost, though.

Sally made toasted ham and cheese sandwiches and they listened to the Gander radio station. At noon CKGA reported that the search for Constable Ross had been delayed due to the weather and would resume as soon as the weather improved.

Sally looked out the window. "Tish, it's stopped snowin'. Please, God, they'll find Terry before dark. I hardly slept all last night – I must have counted every tile in the ceilin' a hundred times. Do you want to take a spin around the harbour? I'd just as soon be doin' somethin' as sittin' here frettin'. We can drop Bette off at Mom and Dad's, they should be home by now."

After the child was handed over to her grandparents, Delmont pointed her car in the direction of the town hall, at Sally's request.

The hall's parking lot was full—a dozen RCMP vehicles, three Search and Rescue cube vans, a large number of residents' cars and trucks. The two large doors of the fire hall were up. People were milling around everywhere. Delmont thought how decent it was for all these people to have come out on such a day for the sake of Terry Ross. Although the cynical side of her was saying they'd have probably come out for a stray cat, considering how boring their lives were. And they had no internal lives.

"Where's the fish plant, Sally?"

"You've never seen the fish plant?"

Sally made it sound like Delmont was a Londoner and she'd never seen the statue of Nelson in Trafalgar Square. "No, I haven't."

Several twists and turns later, Delmont's car was sitting next to a large, nondescript, industrial building by the ocean.

"It's . . . pretty big."

"Yes, it's a large buildin'. There used to be four hundred people workin' the day shift and four hundred on nights in there. Everyone was gettin' fifty or sixty hours a week. Want to drive out on the wharf a little ways?"

"Okay." Not really, the driving was slippery, and she didn't feel like ending up in the North Atlantic. But the wharf was broad and paved – even ploughed. A slight spray of salt-water was passing over the wharf. And her brakes were good. Why not? She was suffering from Setback boredom too. Next, she'd be in a dust-up at Longview.

"Tell me about the big boats."

"They're longliners, some people call them sixty-five-footers. They fish offshore, for mackerel, herrin', flounder, halibut, and crab. Some go out a couple of hundred miles and could be gone for days."

"Sounds dangerous."

"It is, Newfoundland loses a half dozen fishermen every year to the Atlantic Ocean. And some of them are young, with their lives ahead of them. Gone before their time."

"I recently read, "In the Heart of the Sea," by Nathaniel Philbrick. It's about a whaling ship, called the "Essex" lost in the Pacific in 1820. Never knowing I'd ever be living and working next to the ocean."

"Tish, it takes a strong, rough and tough man to leave his

family and go offshore to fish for a living. They're a special breed. They use to hunt seals in the spring of the year when the ice came in. But not many at it anymore, as the quota was cut big time by the federal government because of pressure from international environmentalists. And also, because the price of the pelts has also collapsed."

"I read a big story about the Newfoundland seal hunt a few years back in either the Chicago Tribune or the Sun-Times. I believe it was written by a member of the Sea Shepherd Society, signed by a captain I believe. I don't recall his name."

"Most likely Paul Watson, he is a marine captain and the founder of the Sea Shepherd Conservation Society, which was started in Vancouver, British Columbia, back in the seventies. He was also a co-founder of Greenpeace. But got kicked for being too radical."

"Yes, I believe that was the name."

"Tish, I loves seal meat, especially flippers. I'll have to get Dad to cook you a feed. Dad does a great job of cookin' them. Not everyone can cook them. Every spring when I was growing up, we couldn't wait to get a feed of flippers."

"Thanks, but I'll pass."

"It's delicious!"

"Again, I'll pass!"

They watched a blue boat with white trim leave the wharf. Damn – she wished she had her camera. "Sally. Let's go to my house for coffee."

"We could have coffee at my house."

"I'm not a fan of instant, Sally.'

"I'm not really a fan of coffee."

"There's tea, girl."

They stopped at a convenience store for cream and a box of donuts and then headed to South Side Point Road. As they travelled the road, they noticed the blue boat that they saw leaving the wharf on the other side of town. It was idling opposite the white cross on the bank. Three men on the deck were looking towards the site and pointing. Taking turns with a set of binoculars.

"I don't like that, Tish. What are they doin' out on a day like this, and why are they there? What are they lookin' at?"

"I don't know. Let's watch them for a while."

They watched the men on the boat for ten minutes. Delmont was about to suggest that they keep going to her house when they heard the clattering sound of a helicopter. They looked up: two helicopters were coming in their direction, low and fast.

"Oh, Tish, I told you there was somethin' wrong. I knew it – I knew Terry's car went over the bank. Oh, dear God. Oh, I hope he's still alive."

"Sally, we don't know anything. Come on, let's go to my place and listen to the radio. There might be some news."

And then they saw the vehicles. Five or six, close to the bank with the white cross on it. Most of them had flashing lights. Oh Lord, it wasn't looking good. Though it might turn out well, you never knew. But Delmont was having trouble buying her own optimism. She moved the car closer to the embankment where the lonely cross stood.

A dozen or so men were standing on the road. Two of them were putting on rappelling harnesses. Two ropes had been tied to the guard rail. A minute later, the two wearing the rappelling gear stepped over the guardrail and slowly backed down over the bank and were lost from sight. One had a radio attached to his harness.

Delmont broke the silence. "How did the car get through the guardrail? If there is a car down there."

Sally said in a low emphatic whisper. "There's one openin' in the guardrail."

"Who's driving that Lincoln?" Must be an important man, thought Delmont. That's the kind of car they drove. Men who weren't important drove sports cars. This meant, I may not be important, but I have a big penis.

"That's the mayor. I'm goin' to talk to him. He'll tell me what's goin' on."

Her voice was a bit stronger now. Delmont knew that knowing the worst is usually better than being in the dark. She crossed her fingers underneath the steering wheel.

When Delmont's car approached the emergency vehicles, an RCMP officer flagged them down. Delmont rolled down her window.

"Sorry, this road is closed and might be closed for hours. You can't get through here unless it's an emergency."

Sally leaned over Delmont. "I need to speak to the mayor, officer."

"You'll have to give me your name and tell me what it's about."

"I'm Sally Osmond, the town clerk, and I'm a friend of Terry Ross's."

Obviously, thought Delmont, the Mountie thought Sally meant girlfriend because he didn't question her any further. Instead, he radioed the mayor.

"He says he's on his way. But you may have to wait a while, please back up."

It was half an hour before they saw the mayor walking in their direction. He was obviously cold and partially winded. The weather wasn't being kind to a man like him – middle-aged and overweight.

Delmont got in the back of the two-door so that the mayor could sit beside Sally. He got in behind the steering wheel and wheezed for a full minute before he could speak.

 "Oh my, girls, that wind is somethin' else."

Sally's voice was jagged. "Tell me it's not Terry."

White took her hand. "Sally, we're not sure yet. A boat spotted a car and reported it. They said that a car was at the bottom of the bank, on its roof, wheels up. They couldn't tell if it was a police cruiser or not. It has been burnt. I guess that's why the helicopter pilots never spotted it. It would blend in with the dark grey rocks. Whatever it is, it's only been there for a day, two at the most. We have boats comin' and goin' in and out of this harbour every day. Certainly, someone would have seen it before now. Two Search and Rescue climbers are rappellin' down. We're waitin' on them to report back."

Sally was as silent as the grave. Delmont took over

"If it is Terry Ross, could it have been an accident?"

"Highly unlikely."

"Why?"

"There is only one openin' in the guardrail. It would be too much of a coincidence for him to have gone through it. And neither of the ends of the guardrail is damaged. This location was the dumpin' site for a body years ago. Everyone in the community knows that. And for Terry to be in this area on a Saturday night would be highly unusual. The RCMP comes out here once or twice a week, and never Saturday night – Saturday nights are too busy."

Sally suddenly turned on the radio, just in time to hear the announcer tell them what they already knew: that a car had been found on some rocks by the ocean in Setback, and that the RCMP and Search and Rescue were on site.

A Mountie rapped on the driver's window of Delmont's car. The mayor rolled it down.

"Mayor White, I'm sorry to interrupt, but our commander needs to speak to you immediately."

The mayor turned to Sally. "I'm sorry, my dear, but I have to go. You should go home now. I'll give you a call when we have any news."

"I'm not goin' nowhere until I know if it's Terry." Sally's

voice was small but firm. "Can you tell me one thing before you leave?"

"What's that, Sally?" The mayor looked as uncomfortable as a cow at a barbeque.

"Why didn't anyone see the car on fire?"

"Cars can burn out in five or ten minutes, quicker if an accelerant is used. And we're a half kilometre or more from town. Not many people out this far on either side of the harbour late at night. The car is near the water, and we've had southwest winds until today. The smoke most likely billowed out the harbour. That car could have been there for weeks or months if those fishermen hadn't spotted it. One of the helicopters scoured this part of the coast this mornin' and saw nothin'."

The wind came in like a dagger when the mayor got out. Delmont pushed the seat ahead and placed herself behind the wheel.

Neither one of them spoke. They watched the ocean, where three large boats and four small boats had congregated, rocking in the wind a few hundred feet offshore in the same spot the blue and white boat had been earlier. The boats were tied to one another, bow to stern. The water was smooth in the harbour.

Sally spoke. "Who murdered Terry, Tish? Who?"

Delmont put an arm around the girl. "Sally, this is no good. Why don't I take you home to your parents? You can get something to eat, have a rest. You can't change anything that's happened by sitting here. You can't help Terry. He thought a lot about you – he wouldn't want you to be breaking your heart out here today."

Sally squared her shoulders. "I owe it to him, Tish. He was the only man who's ever been decent to me. I'm sorry I couldn't love him, but I did like him an awful lot." She burst out crying.

"That's it, I'm taking you home." Delmont started up the car. She'd been doing that off and on since they arrived, trying to keep warm. But she wasn't going to turn it off again, she was taking Sally away from this desolate place. Herself, too.

Sally suddenly stopped crying and grabbed Delmont's hand. "No, wait. Look - the climbers are back up. They're gettin' in the Search and Rescue van. Now we'll know. The mayor will come and tell us. He's gettin' in the van now. I bet it's Terry's cruiser and he's in it, dead."

"You don't know that for sure, Sally. Life isn't like a mystery novel. Not very often, anyway."

"It is today, Tish. The climbers are in that van bein' debriefed, and the mayor is in there bein' told what's below the cliff. And it's not a civilian's car. It's Terry Ross's cruiser and he's in it. Dead and burnt." She put her face in her hands.

Five silent minutes, silent except for the music on the radio, later, the mayor walked to their car. Delmont got in the back and gave him the driver's seat.

The mayor didn't seem to want to break the silence. But he knew he had to. He faced Sally and said, "My dear, it is Terry

Ross. He's dead in his car at the bottom of the bank." His voice was hoarse. He cleared his throat.

Sally didn't move or speak.

"I'm sorry, my dear. His body was burnt along with the car. His pistol is not in its holster, and the microphone was torn from his radio. I only hope and pray he was dead before the car was set ablaze. "

Delmont felt like someone had punched her in the gut. She'd never been anywhere near a murder before. This was too close to home, literally and figuratively. She would have to move, take her stuff, and stay in the hotel until it was time to leave Setback. It couldn't be any worse than that awful villa in Italy with the bats.

The mayor licked his chapped lips. "This has to be kept quiet for another hour or two. The RCMP is contactin' the closest detachment to Terry's family in rural Saskatchewan so they can get in touch with his family. His dental records will be couriered overnight from Saskatchewan to the chief pathologist in St. John's so that the body can be officially identified. This is a sad day for the RCMP in this province. Terry is the third RCMP officer to be killed on duty in Newfoundland. Constable John Hoey was killed in Botwood in 1958 – poor fella, he was only twenty-one, just out of trainin'. Constable Robert Amey was killed in 1964 in Whitbourne in a shootout with four men who escaped from Her Majesty's Penitentiary in St. John's."

Delmont wondered if he was going to give them the entire

history of the Mounties in Newfoundland. But he was in shock, she supposed, and that made some people garrulous.

Mayor White put his hand on the car door handle. "I have to leave. We have a debriefin' at the fire hall in twenty minutes."

"How will they get the car and the body up over the cliff?"

"A five-ton boom truck is on its way from Gander - should be here in a few hours. A tow truck wouldn't be able to haul the car up, it's too far down. Also, it's tangly down there with tuckamores and alders. The car has to be brought up slowly and gently. The police do not want any evidence destroyed. I'll keep you girls up to date!" The expression on the mayor's face said he'd rather not.

"We're goin' to Tish's house, mayor. I'll give you her number if you got a piece of paper."

The mayor sighed and removed a notepad from his shirt pocket.

"I guess we got to go back to Tish's, don't we? The road is closed."

"It could be closed for a day or two, but if you need to get home, you can be escorted through."

Thank all the gods, thought Delmont. Although she wasn't looking forward to being alone in an isolated house with a murderer on the loose – and possibly in the vicinity – another couple of hours with Sally was about all she could take. She knew her limits when it came to other people's emotions.

The mayor got out of the car and trundled off and Tish

returned to the driver's seat. She backed up the car, slowly turned around and headed home. Although it had never felt less like home.

Sally sat down heavily on a kitchen chair. She was still imitating a deaf-mute, which was okay by Delmont. Better a deaf-mute than a hysterical woman.

"What can I get you, Sally?"

"Just a cup of tea, Tish. If I eat anythin', it would come right back up. I just can't get my head around it: Terry had his whole life ahead of him, and some low life took it from him over a dead moose or a bag of weed or some woman. Whoever did this, I hope they burn in hell."

"I'll boil the kettle."

"I got to call Mom and Dad, Tish, tell them I'm here with you for a while. I know they're goin' to ask if I heard anythin' about Terry, and I'll have to say no. I hates lyin' to them, never did it before, not once."

Delmont grinned after Sally had turned her back and was heading for the phone. Jesus in his Holy Diaper, how many times had she lied to her own mother? Out of consideration, of course.

Chapter 17

An hour later, after a pot of tea and half a pot of coffee and not much conversation, the phone rang. Delmont answered it and handed the receiver to Sally. "It's Rick." She headed for her bedroom, to give Sally some privacy. And to lie down for five minutes, or however long Sally stayed on the phone. She was bone tired. And no wonder. She woke up to Sally calling her name, and reluctantly went downstairs.

"Sorry, I fell asleep. What did Rick want?"

"Oh, he heard a car went over where Gerry Lyver's car went that time. He wanted to know if I knew if it was Terry's car. He's at Longview, loaded drunk as usual. Listen, Tish, I've been thinkin'. Terry must have been on to somethin' big, like a load of drugs comin' in somewhere along the coast. I mean, I know no one liked him, but no one ever likes cops.

There are hundreds of spots along this coastline where you could smuggle in tons of drugs."

"You might very well be right, Sally."

"The big question is, why run the car over that bank? The same spot as Gerry Lyver went over. Was somone sendin' a message? And how did he die?"

"We'll have to wait for the autopsy, and that will take a few days at least."

"Tish, do you mind if we go back there? The boom truck should have come by now."

Delmont did mind, but she had long ago given up the day as a dead loss. "Of course, we can go back, Sally. Let me fill a couple of thermoses with tea and coffee and we'll head on over."

The site was crawling with men, dark shapes silhouetted against the falling snow. There was a row of emergency vehicles as far as the eye could see, which wasn't far. More boats had joined the fleet in the harbour. Delmont thought she could count ten, but it was hard to tell in such low visibility.

"I guess I was wrong, Tish. The boom truck is not here yet. Maybe we should go back to your place."

"No, Sally, you were right – here it comes now, look"

The long white truck was inching slowly into view, gingerly navigating the traffic, the people and the icy road. The boom truck positioned itself close to the guardrail. Two men from Search and Rescue came out of the van, with large, green oblong bags on their backs. Hands reached out to assist them over the guardrail, and they backed slowly out of sight.

The truck slowly raised its boom and swung it out over the bank. The cable was released, and the hook slowly followed the climbers.

An hour passed. Delmont was tired of turning the car off and on so they wouldn't freeze to death. Their thermoses were empty. Sally seemed to have dozed off. Which was a good thing – she was worn out from shock and grief. And then Delmont saw the truck's cable moving. In reverse: the hook was being reeled back up.

"Sally, wake up."

Sally opened her eyes and yawned. "What is it?"

Delmont pointed. The girl sat up straight and leaned forward. The two of them sat in silence as the truck brought up its grisly prize. There wouldn't be a stuffed animal on the end of this hook, like on the ones at the mall in their glass cases, thought Delmont grimly. Fifteen minutes later, the front of the cruiser crested the bank. As it rose into the air, they could see that the front of it had been burnt a dark grey, almost black. Blue tarpaulins covered the rest of the cruiser's body. Delmont could hear Sally weeping softly; she knew that it had been covered because Terry's body was still inside. The cruiser was slowly lowered onto the flatbed of the truck. The waiting men placed a large, dark green tarp over it. After the tarp was secured to the truck's flatbed, the truck slowly backed up, turned around, and headed in South Side Point Road.

Delmont reached out and tucked a strand of hair, wet from tears, behind Sally's ear.

"Let's go back to my place."

Before she even had her coat off, Sally was on the phone with her father. After she hung up, she told Delmont that she'd filled him in on what had happened and asked him to see if the truck was going to deliver the cruiser to the fire hall. He'd told her he'd drive over there and check and call her back.

"Sally take off your coat. I'm going to heat up some spaghetti unless you'd rather have a sandwich. You need to eat something."

"No, spaghetti's fine, Tish. Only a small plate, though. Oh my God, Tish, Terry's gone. Only twenty-three years old. This was only his second placement. And he was his parents' only son. All they got left is a daughter. I can't bear to think about what they're goin' to go through. I mean, look at me, and I hardly knew him. And to get murdered - they probably wouldn't take it as bad if he'd been sick or got killed in a car accident."

Delmont put two small plates of spaghetti and two glasses of water on the table. "I've dealt with lots of death-induced trauma, Sally, and the grief is the same no matter how the person died. But you're right in a way: They won't be able to get their lives back together until whoever killed Terry is caught."

"Why would they take him to the fire hall?"

"It's the best place to put the cruiser while they take the

body out and put it in a hearse and send it to the Health Sciences Centre in St. John's. The cruiser has to go to St. John's as well, so the forensics crowd can go over it."

The phone rang again.

"It's your father, Sally." Christ in jodhpurs, would she ever have any peace again?

The conversation was short.

"Dad said he didn't see the boom truck, but a hearse was parked in front of the fire hall. And there were at least fifteen emergency vehicles in the parkin' lot. Let's turn on the radio, it's nearly time for the news."

Tish turned on the stereo. Ten minutes later, the news came on, with a report on the finding of Terry Ross's body.

Delmont turned the radio off. "Sally, I'm not trying to get rid of you, but don't you think you need to go home and spend some time with Bette? Get your mind off all this, at least for a little while?"

"Yes, Tish, I do. But my head is goin' round and round like that old weathervane on the Nagles' barn. I wish I knew who done this."

"Sally, it could take many months or years to solve Terry's murder. And some murders are never solved. In the US, nearly a third of murders aren't."

"It didn't take them years to find Gerry Lyver's killer. That was solved in a week or two."

"Well, they were lucky. Every homicide is different. There

are many, many questions with every murder case. Why was he killed? How was he killed? Who had a motive for killing him? The list goes on and on."

"I want to see whoever killed Terry locked up and left to rot in a prison cell for the maximum time allowed under the law."

The phone rang again. Delmont didn't even bother to pick it up. "It's got to be for you, Sally."

It was.

"That was Rick. He said he heard they'd found Terry's body. That even if he was a big prick, no one had the right to kill him. Nice brother I got, hey? Rick was wonderin' if the person who killed Terry might be the same person who slashed his tires here that night. I said he had a point, he said he had a lot of good points, and I said only when you're sober. He said in that case, he never had any good points today."

"Drunk again, hey?"

"He's always drunk. Wastin' his life away, drunk more than he's sober."

Delmont decided she was really going to try to do something for Sally's brother. Starting with his GP. Starting next week.

"You know, Tish, my bet is on one of the Grant brothers. Or even all of them. One is a convicted murderer, and all three have bad tempers. All three have been poachin' big game and illegally jiggin' codfish."

Sally obviously wasn't in any hurry to leave. Delmont decided she might as well get in on the conversation. "And then there's Rock McGee. You told me that someone told you that he said to Terry after the fight that he wasn't finished with him."

"That was Dad. He heard it down to the Legion. Yeah, Rock is mean enough and nuts enough to be a killer. And all those guys hated Terry, and no one seemed to have had any time for him. Remember what Jimmy Parsons said about Terry on the way home from the club last night." Sally oddly looked at Delmont. "I don't suppose Jimmy could have done somethin' like that, could he?"

Delmont laughed. "In my personal and professional opinion, Sally, it is highly unlikely that Jimmy Parsons would kill a mouse. But you never know – as my mother always said, it's the quiet ones you have to watch out for. I think Terry was onto something criminal, and whoever did it was among the criminal element in Setback." So, who did that leave out, Delmont wondered? Rock McGee, Jimmy Parsons, and Sally's brother?

"Yes. But which one of them? Maybe he told someone – another Mountie, his superior maybe. Sergeant Campbell. Or maybe he left notes or somethin'. Oh, I hope he did. And I wish I knew how he died. I hate to think of him burnin' up in that car."

"Then don't think about it." Delmont suddenly realized

that Sally could probably use a little counselling herself. A bit of behaviour modification wouldn't go astray. She could teach the girl how to get control of her emotions. But did Sally want to? Setback positively seethed with unleashed emotions. It was one of the few ways they had of entertaining themselves.

Chapter 18

When Delmont arrived at the town hall the following morning, it was as quiet as a funeral home on night shift. Not a soul around, for once. She decided to drop in to see Sally first thing if the girl was even in.

She was, and as excited as a dog with two bones.

"Tish! Oh my, the messages on my machine! There's usually only one or two, but today, well! It's full, and the phone hasn't stopped ringin'. Seven were from media, right from St. John's to Saskatchewan. I asked the mayor what to do about them all, and he's goin' to draft a press release."

Before she had finished speaking, the mayor came into her office. He handed Sally a hand-written press release. "Type this up for me, would you please, Sally, and fax it off to all the media outlets that called here today. And if any of them gets back to you and says they want an interview with me, give them my phone number. Oh dear, what a shemozzle."

Delmont excused herself and went back to her office. She discovered that her phone was full of messages as well. Most of them were from women, worried, no doubt, about their children and other loved ones now that there was a murderer on the loose. Well, that was her job: to use her education and experience to ease mental torment. But seeing people individually would be time consuming, and she might not be able to reach everyone who needed her. She decided to call Terry Ross's boss, Sergeant Campbell.

"Hello, Dr. Delmont, what can I do for you? Terrible what happened to young Ross. I understand you were a friend of his."

Crap. Next, she would find herself on a list of suspects. The scorned woman or something. "No, not really. He was a friend of Sally Osmond's. The three of us went out to dinner once."

"Sally. She's a sweet girl. She must be having a hard time with all this."

"Yes, she is. Sergeant, I've had several requests today from people suddenly wanting to see me. Mostly women. I'm pretty sure it's about Terry's murder. Specifically, about the fact that there seems to be a murderer on the loose in Setback. If I agree to see them all, it will take up an enormous amount of my time. And I'm not sure how useful I would be to them, either. I was thinking we should call a town meeting to discuss what happened, and you and Mayor White could reassure the townspeople that things are under control."

"That's a great idea. I'll talk to the mayor and get back to you."

"Great, thanks."

An hour later, Campbell called her back.

"Dr. Delmont. Mayor White is on board with your suggestion. He agrees a meeting should be called. We've scheduled one for two o'clock at the parish hall tomorrow, and it should involve not only the people of Setback but residents from all the surrounding communities. Sally is going to take care of getting the word out."

"God, Sergeant, where will we fit them all?"

Campbell laughed. He had a nice laugh, deep and broad. "Don't worry, only a few dozen will show. This isn't our first rodeo. I'll see you tomorrow. Just sorry it couldn't be in better circumstances."

Delmont and Sally ate lunch in the kitchenette. Sally had brought some of her mother's partridgeberry preserve, which had what Sally called a "deadly" reputation in Setback. Delmont hoped that deadly didn't refer to botulism.

"How did you sleep, Sally?" But she already knew. The girl had bags as big as plums under her eyes.

"I hardly slept at all. Every time I closed my eyes, I saw Terry's face. Life is so unfair, Tish. He had so much to live for."

"Yes, he did, poor kid. Sally, Sergeant Campbell, the

mayor and I are going to hold a meeting tomorrow afternoon at the parish hall. As you probably already know. I've gotten a lot of calls for counselling, and I'm sure they're all to do with Terry's murder. It would take me the rest of my life to deal with them, so I asked Campbell to talk to the mayor about having a public meeting. I'm sure the three of us can reassure the populace, at least a little. It's very stressful, having a murderer on the loose, especially in a small place like Setback. Listen, Sally, if you can't sleep tonight, call me, okay?"

"Thanks, Tish – I'll try a hot toddy, some hot rum and milk. That should work, though I don't like the taste of rum at all."

The wind was blowing hard, out of the west this time, when Tish arrived at the parish hall. Sergeant Campbell had been right: there were only twenty cars or so in the parking lot. Inside, there were about forty people, not including her and Campbell and the mayor. Even though the turnout was low, the meeting would serve its purpose: the few that were there would spread the word in no time.

The mayor opened the meeting. "Good day, folks, and thank you very much for comin'. Our purpose here today – mine, Dr. Delmont's, and Sergeant Campbell's – is, of course, to tell you what is happenin' concernin' the tragic death of Constable Terry Ross of the Royal Canadian Mounted Police, and how we are goin' about keepin' Setback and its environs safe in the aftermath. Here is Sergeant Campbell."

"Thank you, Mayor White. Well, folks, I'm sure you've heard that Constable Terry Ross lost his life in the line of duty here in Setback, sometime early Sunday morning. A young man, just starting out, this is indeed, a terrible tragedy, for him, his family, his RCMP family, and you, the people of Setback. And it is made even more tragic by the circumstances of his death. As you have probably gathered, Constable Ross was murdered."

The audience sucked in their collective breath.

"Constable Ross last contacted the 911 dispatcher at 2:55 a.m. Sunday morning, while doing a traffic check here in Setback. The person he pulled over has spoken with the RCMP and has been cleared as a suspect. After that traffic check, he no longer responded to requests from the dispatcher. By six o'clock, a small local search team assembled and searched for Constable Ross and his cruiser, without success. Just after daylight on Sunday, a Search and Rescue helicopter arrived from Gander, picked up our local fire chief, and commenced an air search. At eight, a full-on local search and rescue effort was put in place, involving our local search and rescue unit, the volunteer fire department, and residents.

As you now know, Constable Ross's body was found at the bottom of a gulch on South Side Point Road. The remains were removed to the Health Sciences Centre in St. John's. The autopsy was completed at noon today.

Constable Ross was killed with a single shot to the back of the head, most likely with his own gun. The bullet removed from his body weighed the same as a .38 special bullet, the .38 special revolver is standard issue for the RCMP. The bullet is en route to a crime lab in Halifax for verification. His pistol has not been found. Divers are searching for it right now."

The hall was as quiet as a church; quieter, even. No coughing or shuffling of feet. Delmont looked at the faces, solemn as those of funeral mourners.

"The RCMP's Major Crimes Unit will be handling this investigation, and it will be aided by members of the Royal Newfoundland Constabulary. Expect to have police officers knocking on your doors, but don't be unduly concerned. Only the guilty need to be worried. Are there any questions?"

A middle-aged man stood up, twisting his wool hat in both hands. "Sir, as you doubtless knows, we had another murder in Setback some years ago where the body ended up in the same gulch. Is it your opinion that the two murders are connected?"

Campbell replied, "It is much too early in the investigation to know that, or much else. The main message I have for you today is that you should lock your doors and be wary of going out alone, but also that the murder was likely a targeted one and the killer probably doesn't present a threat to the rest of you. But err on the side of caution. There will be a strong police presence in Setback for the foreseeable future, which should deter further criminal activity."

A large woman with a furrowed brow got up. "Sir, I hates

to say this, but no one had any time for Constable Ross. Not that he should have been killed or anythin', but there's a lot of hard cases in Setback and God knows which one of them disliked him even more than the rest of us, enough to do away with him. How long is it goin' to take you to find that person or persons?"

Sergeant Campbell frowned and cleared his throat. "I'm well aware that some people in places such as Setback harbour resentment towards members of the RCMP. Small towns are notoriously clannish, and some types of crime are often overlooked because people are related to or neighbours of the criminals. Poaching, for instance. But murder is in a different category, and whatever you felt about Constable Ross, I am asking you to put that aside and do your civic duty. If you think you have seen something or heard something or even just suspect something pertaining to this murder, please come to the detachment. If you are uncomfortable about being seen going into the detachment, arrangements can be made for one of the officers to meet with you somewhere else in an unmarked vehicle. Or you can voice your concerns or suspicions over the phone. Now, Dr. Delmont has a few words to say."

Delmont reiterated the reasons she had been hired to work in Setback and gave her usual spiel about the benefits of counselling and her availability. She told the assembled group that although her mandate did not technically include trauma stemming from Constable Ross's murder, she would extend that mandate to include it. After all, it was an extra burden for Setback, on top of the burdens they were already carrying on account of the collapse of the fishery, and some people might find one more burden too much to bear. She was only too glad to help them if she could.

The first thing Delmont did when she got back to the town hall was go in search of Sally. She found her in the kitchenette, having a cup of tea and some of her mother's "deadly" jam on a piece of toast. The girl looked up when Delmont walked in, a smile on her face. It fell off when she saw Delmont's face.

"Sally, I wish there was an easier way to tell you this, but I can't think of one. Terry was killed by a bullet to the back of his head. And his pistol is missing."

Chapter 19

THREE DAYS AFTER THE MURDER, SERGEANT JENKINS OF THE RCMP's Major Crimes Unit brought the first person in for questioning. Rock McGee refused to answer most of their questions and was rude and belligerent. He admitted to disliking Constable Terry Ross and threatening him after their fight and that he would talk to them again only if he had a lawyer present.

The investigators poured over Gerry Lyver's file. There were obvious similarities. Both victims had been killed in their cars. Both cars had been set on fire and pushed into the same gulch. Had Walter Grant struck again? Or one of the other Grant brothers? Were the Grants stupid enough to murder Ross the same way Lyver was killed? Was someone trying to set the Grants up?

Whatever the Grants had done or not done, they seemed to

have disappeared from Setback. Sergeant Jenkins had been informed that the brothers owned a cabin in over the ridge and organized a helicopter trip for himself and Constable Hogan, who had accompanied him to Setback from St. John's. The fire chief, Jim Grandy, went with the two officers: he knew where all the cabins over the ridge were situated.

The day was sunny and still, the temperature was a few degrees above zero. The chopper landed like a monstrous dragonfly on a frozen marsh close to the cabin, which was a five-minute walk away through snow-shrouded trees. Although the snow on the trail had been packed down by snowmobiles, Jenkins noted that they could have used snowshoes.

Jenkins walked cautiously to the door of the rough wooden structure, knocked, and waited a full minute. He turned the knob and gently opened it. The cabin was vacant. He gestured to the other two.

Hogan touched the stove. "It's cold."

"Guess they haven't been around for a while, if at all. Are there any other cabins near here, Grandy?"

"Yes, about two kilometres to the north." Grandy, a slim, silver-haired man in his fifties, hated flying, especially in helicopters. He had assumed they would be returning to Setback, but Jenkin's next words disabused him of that notion.

"Well, we'd better check them out."

The three men climbed in the chopper and Jenkins told the pilot to head north. Minutes later, Grandy pointed to a small clearing with another snow-covered wooden structure in the middle of it. The pilot found another spot of frozen marsh and landed.

"Rick Osmond owns this one," Grandy said as they got to the clearing in the woods.

Osmond's cabin was vacant as well.

Jenkins picked up a newspaper. "Well, someone's been here since Ross was killed, according to the date on this. Maybe the Grants holed up in this cabin for a night or two, who knows? No one locks their doors around here, apparently. Maybe the Grants have taken turns hiding all over the place – who's going to know? And if someone came across them, they may or may not call the snitch line. I'll take this paper with me, anyway. Might need it for prints later. Grandy, is there another cabin nearby?"

"Yeah, it belongs to the Nagle brothers. Another two kilometres further in, to the north." More flying. He wished he'd gone to his GP for sedatives. He'd used up half his supply getting to the Dominican Republic and back with his wife last year. And the rest had disappeared right after he'd got home. He suspected his son of selling them at the school, but he wasn't ready to confront him just yet. Maybe he'd tell his wife and let her deal with Alf. But the poor frigger wouldn't have a testicle left if she did.

"We've had some information on the Nagles – enough to warrant checking them out. We've been to their house, but they were never in. Lots of that going around in Setback."

The Nagles' cabin proved to be equally empty. Grandy was happy. He'd soon be sitting at the diner with a huge mug of coffee and a plate of donuts on the table in front of him. He had one of those metabolisms - no matter how much he ate, it just never stuck to his ribs. His wife resented this enormously.

The flight back to Setback was uneventful. Jenkins and Hogan went to a local café with Grandy and had some lunch.

"I guess we should try Longview. We might be able to flush the Grants out there."

Hogan looked at his superior officer. He didn't relish a trip to the place he'd heard the locals called the Swamp. Nasty things lived in swamps.

Rock McGee was on the bar when the officers walked in.

"Hello, Mr. McGee. Could you tell us if William, Walter or Michael Grant has been in here in the past few days?"

McGee kept his eyes on the bar. "Never seen 'em this long time."

"Are you sure?"

McGee looked up and sneered. "Yes, I'm sure, I'm here every day, seven days a week."

Outside Longview, the wind had begun to assert its authority, whipping snow into small drifts, and sticking cold fingers down the back of the officer's jackets.

"He's never going to give us anything, the prick. Maybe

because he doesn't have anything, maybe because he's just a prick. Let's go get a coffee, Hogan."

Hogan thought about all the local pricks they'd been given information about and would have to interview. Oh well, at least that pretty girl at the café made a wicked, as they said here, cup of coffee. None better in all of Halifax, his hometown.

Ten days after the murder, a reward of $5,000 was offered for information leading to the arrest and prosecution of the person or persons responsible for the murder of Constable Terry Ross. A phone line for anonymous tips was set up. If anyone wanted to speak to an officer, one was available at all times. It wasn't long before the line was in use. Apparently, almost everyone in Setback had an opinion on who killed Ross.

The Grant brothers' names came up often, along with Rock McGee's. The Nagle brothers were popular as well. One man said he was sure his ex-wife had a hand in it as "She was after him like a bitch in heat, b'ys, and he would never have nothin' to do with her." Several people said they'd seen a mysterious stranger in town around the time of the murder. The list grew longer as the days passed. The investigation team was kept busier than vampires at a blood bank. It seemed as though half the men in Setback were on their list.

Sally was coming out of the town hall when Sergeant Jenkins stopped her.

"Ms. Osmond, how are you? We haven't met, but I've

seen you coming and going. I'm Sergeant Jenkins of the Major Crimes Unit. Do you have a moment? I'd like to speak with you."

"Certainly, Sergeant. Did you want to go into my office?"

"No, Ms. Osmond, I can walk to your car with you – I guess you're on your way home? – and tell you what I have to say on the way."

Sally had an unpleasant feeling in her stomach. What did this police officer want with her? Oh, well, it couldn't be anything much – probably something to do with work, with the town hall.

"Ms. Osmond, we have informed your brother that we'd like to interview him concerning the murder of Terry Ross -"

"My brother? Rick? Oh no, Sergeant, oh no – not Rick. Rick could never, ever –"

"Ms. Osmond, I am telling you this simply as a courtesy, because your work has you assisting the police from time to time, and because the mayor was concerned that what I just said would upset you unduly. And it has. But it shouldn't. We are interviewing nearly everyone in town, it seems. Someone left your brother's name on the tip line. I guess he's got an enemy or two. Everyone has. That tip line is a reservoir of old grudges. So, don't worry, Ms. Osmond, I'm confident that this case will be solved fairly quickly and then we'll be out of your hair and life can return to normal."

Sally's legs felt like jelly. She held on to her car as she

watched Jenkins walk back to the detachment office. She had to talk to Tish. Thank God she was working late.

Delmont was just hanging up the phone when Sally burst into her office.

"Tish, Tish! Oh my God, Tish, you'll never believe –" Sally was sobbing now, the tears streaming.

Delmont bit the inside of her lip. Christ in a hammock, what was wrong with the girl now? Her mother's homemade bread fail to rise? Her father's new pants too big for him?

"Sit down, Sally – take a few deep breaths. That's it. Now, tell me about it."

"One of the RCMP officers – I'm that upset I can't even remember his name – caught up with me when I was leavin' work and told me they were bringin' Rick in for questionin' about Terry's murder. Oh, Tish – Rick wouldn't hurt a fly. Oh, this is goin' to kill Mom and Dad!"

Rick Osmond, a suspect? Delmont wondered where the RCMP had come up with that one. The investigation must have hit a wall. And then she remembered the source of this information.

"Sally, are you sure? Is that all he said? Just walked up to you and said that your brother is a murder suspect? Why would they even talk to you about it?"

"Because I work in the buildin' and assist them occasionally, and the mayor told them I might be upset when I found out they were questionin' Rick. The officer said not to be upset because everyone in town was callin' that tip line they have set up and sayin' everythin' about everybody. Someone left a message on the tip line and told them to talk to Rick. He said they had to talk to everyone that was mentioned." She took a deep breath and then smiled. "I don't think he was lookin' forward to that."

"Well, there you go. There is nothing to be upset about, Sally. They have to follow protocol, that's all."

"I guess so. And he did say everyone has one or two enemies, and that's who he figured called Rick in. And I guess my brother does know a few people who don't like him. He's got an awful mouth on him when he's drinkin', and he's always drinkin'."

"Or maybe the police think he might have heard something. Or that whoever gave them Rick's name might be trying to deflect attention from himself, maybe a person involved himself. Maybe they'll get Rick to give them a few names. Go home and forget about it, girl."

"I'm goin' over to Mom and Dad's – they must be out of their minds about this. Oh, poor Rick."

Sally pulled her handbag off the arm of the chair and stood up. Then she turned to Delmont with a startled look on her face. "Tish – I just thought about somethin'. What if Rick sauces the cops when they're talkin' to him? He probably will, too. Oh, dear Jesus, they'll put him in the lockup for sure. And my parents will never get over it. No one in our family has ever been in trouble with the law – oh, Tish!"

Straight to death. Delmont felt like shaking Sally until her teeth rattled, although that had never been proven to have any therapeutic efficacy. Not for the patient, anyway, but maybe for the therapist. "Sally stop it! You need some behaviour modification. You need to get some control over your thought processes, so you won't end up in this endless loop of drama and negativity all the time. Do you want me to help you with that? I can."

Sally looked at Delmont as if she'd slapped her. "Are you sayin' I'm cracked? That I have mental health problems?"

"No, Sally. Not serious ones, anyway. Lots of people have mental quirks that make them unhappy, and that we therapists can sometimes do something about. I just hate to see you suffer for nothing, that's all."

"It's not nothin', Tish – you don't know Rick."

Delmont got up and put her arms around the girl. "No, I don't. And I'm sorry. If you need me, just call, okay?"

After Sally had left, Delmont mentally chastised herself for being insensitive. A night in the lockup in Delmont's milieu would just be the subject of a funny story, but in Setback, with its small town values, it could be the basis of social ostracization for a family like Sally's. Or if not that, at the very least her parents would take the shame to their graves. City life had its own problems, but morality wasn't one of them.

Thirty minutes after Tish got home from work, her phone rang. She wondered why Sally would call from her parents' house – had there been a new development?

"Hello, Sally. What's up?"

"It's Sergeant Jenkins of the RCMP, Dr. Delmont. I'd like to interview you about Constable Ross's murder. Would you prefer that interview to take place at the detachment, or your home?"

Damn, damn, damn. Delmont had hoped for some time off from the never-ending drama of Terry Ross and his sorry fate. "Depends on when you want to conduct it."

"We were hoping to speak to you this evening, ma'am. Time is of the essence in a case like this."

Quadruple damn. "Fine. You can come to the house. What time?"

"What about an hour from now? We can send an unmarked car."

"Okay." As if unmarked cars weren't as obvious as marked ones, in their own way. But at least she'd have an hour to relax.

Two RCMP officers arrived exactly an hour later. Two men of indeterminate age and looks. The caller identified himself as Sergeant Jenkins; the shorter officer was Constable Hogan. She invited them in and offered tea or coffee. The shorter of the officers replied.

"No, thank you, ma'am, but it's kind of you to offer. We'd like to get right down to why we're here."

"I suspect it's to ask me about Constable Ross getting his tires slashed here a few weeks ago."

"That is correct. That's one of the issues. Would you mind telling us about what happened that night?"

"Sally Osmond, Terry Ross, and I went to dinner at Hong's restaurant at approximately six o'clock. We were there until around eight, and then we came back here for a drink. We had a drink, and at about ten o'clock Terry said he had to go home to let his dog out, but that he could come back for coffee afterwards. He and Sally left the house in her car but came back shortly afterwards. Terry said someone had slashed all four of his tires, while they were gone."

The taller of the two officers took over. "Dr. Delmont, did you or Constable Ross or Ms. Osmond hear anyone outside during the time the three of you spent in this house? A car, footsteps, voices? Anything?"

"No, nothing. We were here in the living room, with the radio on, and we were having a fairly animated conversation."

"I see. Do you remember what this conversation was about?"

"God, no. Well, yes. It was about nothing, really. The weather, life. Casual stuff."

"How well did you know Constable Ross?"

"Not well at all. That was the only time I was in his company, really. He was Sally's friend."

"You work in the same building with Ms. Osmond. Would you say the two of you are friends?"

"Yes, I would."

"So, are you able to tell us what the relationship between

Ms. Osmond and Constable Ross was – you said friends, but are you sure it wasn't more than that? A romantic relationship, perhaps?"

Oh, Christ with a lollipop. "I think perhaps it was heading that way, but I really can't say for sure. They'd gone for drives – Sally and Terry and Sally's daughter, Bette. But as far as I'm aware, that night was the first time she'd been with him in public. And I was there too, so it wasn't exactly a date." There wouldn't have been any real dates for Sally with Terry Ross, but she wasn't about to tell them that. It wasn't relevant to the investigation.

"Sally Osmond is Rick Osmond's sister. Do you know Rick Osmond? Has he ever been to you for counselling?"

"I don't know him well, and, no, he hasn't been to see me professionally. He came here twice to drop off firewood, and I've run into him at Sally's. Like a lot of men in this community, he's been adversely affected by the closure of the fishery."

"Can you be more specific?"

"About what?"

"Mr. Osmond. How would you describe him?"

"Rick? An average young man who has had his livelihood taken from him. He is unhappy about this, naturally." And that is all you're getting from me, coppers. You don't need to go chasing after Rick Osmond when there's a seriously psychopathic killer on the loose.

The two men looked at each other and then back at

Delmont. She realized they knew she was holding back, but too bad. Whatever she could tell them about Rick didn't add up to anything they could use.

"Dr. Delmont, you realize that withholding information about a serious crime is against the law? Even when something is told to you professionally, in confidence"

"Yes, I am well aware of that."

"So, Mr. Osmond has never spoken to you about Constable Ross?"

"No." Delmont was good at poker, fortunately. She hated lying, but in this case, it was justified. Whatever Rick had said to her out of his drunken hatred of the world in general and Terry Ross in particular, was not going to aid these men. And it could hurt Sally and her family if it ever got out. And things always get out.

"One last question: have you ever had any dealings with Rock McGee or the Grant brothers?"

"Only peripherally. I know who McGee is, and I saw him once or twice when Sally and I went to the Longview Lounge. Bill Grant was a patient of mine, and also delivered firewood here once. He said nothing in the course of our counselling or on the one occasion he was here that has any bearing on this case. He made no mention of the police at all. I was treating him for depression related to the fishery closure."

"You say he was your patient. Does that mean you are no longer treating him?"

"No. I've referred him to a colleague in St. John's who is

a better fit for him."

Again, the two men exchanged glances. Let them. Delmont was not about to give them anything they didn't need.

"Well, Dr. Delmont, that's all we need for now. If we have any questions, we think you might be able to answer down the road, we'll be in touch. Thank you for your cooperation."

"You're most welcome."

Later, in a full tub with candles on the windowsill above it and a glass of vermouth by the side, Delmont let her mind slide over the murder. Who had done it? There were a lot of contenders in this strange, savage little town. Well, she'd be gone soon, perhaps even before the murder was solved. She'd probably keep in touch with Sally for a while afterwards and might eventually find out who did it. Not that she cared terribly. This summer she was going to Iceland with Jenny and Noel, a couple of old friends. Iceland was exotic in a cold, savage way as well. Vikings were one thing Newfoundland and Iceland had in common. It took tough people to survive in both places. Although Iceland was literate and civilized from what she'd read. What had happened to Newfoundland? Perhaps it had something to do with the ancestral stock, Scandinavian versus English and Irish. But she was too tired to think of that, or anything else.

Chapter 20

"How did you sleep last night, Sally?" Delmont had barely gotten her coat off when Sally appeared at her office door. Asking was merely a courtesy. Delmont already knew what the girl would answer by her face, wan and bruised looking under the eyes.

"Not good. I may have gotten a few hours. And to top it all off, Rick hasn't been home to sleep the last few nights. My parents are worried to death about him. Not only hasn't he come home, but two RCMP officers were over to mom and dad's twice, lookin' for him. And now they want to talk to me."

"That's too bad, Sally. I'm sorry you're going through all this. It probably won't go on much longer. Just answer their questions when they interview you. Short and to the point. That's all you're required to do.

Speaking of the police, two RCMP officers were at my place last night, asking about the night Terry's tires were slashed. And about Rock McGee and the Grant brothers. I told them what I could, but there wasn't much to tell. And they asked me about Rick, but there's no need for you to know that."

"Oh my. That must have stressed you right out?"

"No. I've had to deal with the police before, Sally."

"You never told me that."

"There's not much to tell." Delmont felt her guts tighten: the trauma of what the police had put her through when Ruth died lived right there still, right in her guts. Right between her heart and her pelvis.

Sergeant Jenkins' team was going around in circles. They couldn't find either of the Grant brothers. The Grant brothers were the only people in Setback that they had collected enough evidence on – circumstantial and unrelated to the case though most of it was – to proceed with. They had followed up on any tip from the snitch line that had some meat on its bones, and several that didn't. They had pored over files and considered histories and characters. Some days it seemed as though almost every single person in Setback had been weighed and measured when it came to murder. This one, anyway. And then there was always the possibility of the murderer being someone who was just passing through. Jenkins had even had a nightmare about that.

Ten days had passed, and they had nothing to show for their relentless pursuit of the killer. They had even talked to the wife of the man who allegedly had been like "a bitch in heat" after Ross. All Jenkins and Hogan had gotten out of that interview was a collection of Newfoundland off-colour expressions. Very interesting, but not useful. Not to the murder inquiry, anyway, although Hogan resolved to use them on his buddies when he went home to Halifax. He'd even written down the ones he could remember. Such as "Ye two fuckin' skeets, get out of me house before I rips off yer heads and sticks them up yer fuckin' arses." His two young nephews would get a kick out of that one. And he'd get a kick too, if his sister, their mother, caught him telling her sons naughty words. But she'd never caught him yet.

Jenkins said to Hogan, "Maybe we should get warrants for the Grants. Besides the fact that Walter Grant is a convicted murderer, there is, as you know, evidence that Constable Ross was about to break their poaching operation open. That's not enough to go in with, but I hear the JP in Gander signs warrants blindfolded. That's what Campbell says, anyway."

"Maybe. But before we waste even more time doing that, let's take one more trip to Bill Grant's house. If we take him into custody, the other two might cave in."

Jenkins approached Grant's grey saltbox house with a heavy heart. All they were going to get here, likely, was what they got the last time. His skinny, sour wife telling them she hadn't seen her husband in days and had no idea where he was.

The door opened, and Jenkins could feel his eyebrows shooting up. According to the description Campbell had given him, this man was surely Bill Grant.

"Hello, Mr. Grant. I'm Sergeant Jenkins of the RCMP and this is Constable Hogan. May we come in?"

Grant leered at Jenkins. The stink of old sweat and fresh alcohol made the police officer back up a step.

"I was expectin' you earlier than this. What took you b'ys so long?"

"Mr. Grant, we would like you to come to the detachment and answer a few questions about the murder of Constable Terry Ross." Jenkins wondered what it would take to get him down there: whatever it was, they were prepared to do it.

"Sure, why not? Come in while I hauls on me coat and boots."

Jenkins looked at Hogan. His eyebrows were up around his hairline too. The two officers entered the house and followed Grant to the kitchen. It was as spick and span as a model kitchen in a magazine, you could eat off the floor, thought Jenkins. It looked like Grant's wife put all her affection into her home. God knew there was no point wasting it on her husband, from what he'd heard about the man.

Grant noticed the officers looking around from the daybed where he was putting on a pair of green rubber boots. "That's right – there isn't a cleaner house in Setback. The wife's a good baker too – too bad she's gone for groceries or else I'd get her to make you a cup of tea and give you a slice of her homemade bread. No store-bought garbage in this house."

"Mr. Grant, before we head to the detachment, can you tell us where your brothers are?"

"What, the b'ys playin' hide-and-seek with you or what?" Grant dirtied the clean white kitchen with a nasty laugh.

"I'll ask you one more time, Mr. Grant. Where are your brothers?"

"No need gettin' on like that, me son. They're up to the cabin."

"In that case, Mr. Grant, I'm afraid you may have to be our overnight guest at the detachment if we can't bring your brothers in today. Maybe you and your brothers are a little too good at hide-and-seek, eh?"

After they'd settled Grant away in a cell – during which officer Hogan obtained some new words for his Newfoundland cursing file - Jenkins contacted RCMP headquarters in St. John's and asked them to send a helicopter from Gander. It was 2 p.m. Not many hours of light were left on this dull, cloudy winter day. Headquarters said they could get one there within the hour or so. That would work: the cabin was only a ten-minute run, but if the Grants were there and they had to take them back, the pilot would probably not have time to get back to Gander. They could put him up in Setback at what passed for a hotel.

The helicopter had been circling for several minutes over the area where Jenkins was positive the cabins would be. But there was no sign of the cabins. Jenkins cursed himself for not bringing the fire chief with them. It was all woods and bogs, and everything looked the same. And the snow that had fallen the night before wasn't helping. He directed the pilot to where he thought the Nagles' cabin was, but there was no sign of that one either. Goddamn it! He was getting claustrophobic out here. It was like being trapped in some kind of maze. Thank God they weren't on snowmobiles. He'd never seen a landscape that was so inhospitable to humans in his life. Maybe way up north there was one, but he'd never been up north, and now that he had seen this, he did not have any desire to go up there. The chopper circled around for five minutes, making broader and broader arcs until he knew they were off course. Well, he'd tell the pilot to go where he thought Rick Osmond's cabin was, and if that one had been miraculously carried off by the fairies, they'd head back. It was nearly twilight anyway.

At least Osmond's cabin had stayed put. The light was rapidly dimming, but he could see a white hump with darker bits here and there that he assumed was Osmond's snow-covered place. He told the pilot to go back to Setback.

Back at the detachment, Jenkins explained about the

disappearing cabins. He suggested that the phenomenon was likely due to the heavy snowfall of the night before. Either that or they'd been completely off course, which was possible but unlikely since Osmond's cabin had been found. In any case, they'd take the fire chief with them the next morning when they went back in over the ridge. Jenkins had asked the pilot if he could take them up early the next morning, and he'd said he could. He'd have to cover the chopper with a tarp, however – freezing rain had been forecast.

Campbell called the mayor and asked if he could get some members of the volunteer fire department to obtain tarpaulins and assist the pilot in covering the helicopter. The mayor said he'd make a call to the chief immediately.

Chapter 21

THE NEXT MORNING THE SUN, PARTLY OBSCURED BY CLOUDS, did its best to shine on the snow covered ball field in Setback where the helicopter had spent the night. Volunteer firemen who covered the chopper the previous evening removed the tarpaulins. The pilot, Jenkins, Hogan, and the fire chief climbed aboard. The pilot engaged the engine, and they were soon airborne. Jenkins wished he'd brought earplugs.

He watched as ten minutes of bog-woods-bog passed under them in all of its monotony. Then he heard Grandy speak.

"Down there – it's down there." Grandy was pointing downward as he spoke. "Well, I can't see it, but that's where it should be. Set her down on the nearest bog, and we'll walk into that grove of trees. The cabin has to be in there somewhere."

It was a slog. The snow was deeper than it looked from the air, although it had been somewhat packed down by snowmobiles.

"I can smell somethin' burnin'." Grandy had his neck stretched out and his nose in the air like a pointer.

Jenkins and Hogan could too. And around the next bend in the trail, they discovered what it was. The remains of the Grants' cabin, still smouldering under its blanket of snow.

"Christ. No wonder we couldn't find it yesterday."

"Sir, I wonder if there are bodies in there."

"I doubt it, Hogan. I'm willing to bet good money that the Grants burned it down themselves. I don't think there are any bodies in that pile of burned wood, but I wouldn't be surprised if there wasn't evidence of several crimes. Maybe even the smoking gun."

Hogan grinned, but then he realized that Jenkins wasn't even smiling. Of course, it wasn't a joke. Jenkins had a sense of humour, but not that kind. Hogan hadn't quite figured out what kind yet.

"Maybe they're holed up in the Nagles' cabin. Let's try there."

When they flew over the location of Nagles' cabin, they could see that it had also been burnt to the ground. They landed and trudged through the deep snow to the pile of burnt lumber.

"What the hell is going on here?"

"I don't know, sir. But something is, for sure." Hogan

sniffed the air. He liked the scent of burning wood. It reminded him of Christmas at his grandmother's. She lived out in Annapolis Valley and had a big wood stove.

"Well, we'd better get back to the detachment and figure out where to go from here."

Grandy didn't think he'd ever heard sweeter words. The chopper lifted into the air and hovered for a moment. Then, as the pilot was about to set course for Setback, something appeared in Jenkins' peripheral vision. Smoke.

"Hogan, Grandy, look over there. Looks like our arsonist has struck again. See that smoke?"

"Yes, sir." Hogan saw it. Looked just like the smoke that came out of his grandmother's chimney and snaked over the apple trees in her backyard.

Grandy cleared his throat. "Actually, I believe that smoke is comin' from a chimney, Alan. There's a difference between smoke comin' from a burnin' buildin' and smoke from a chimney, even at this distance. I know smoke - smoke and fire are my line of work."

"Set the helicopter down as close as you can get to that smoke, Paul. We're going to talk to Rick Osmond, see what he knows about the fires. He's overdue for a chat, anyway. Remember? Someone called in anonymously about Rick. Said he was a drug dealer. Not that I'm taking that too seriously. Probably bullshit, or if it is true, nickel and dime stuff. If he were a big player, the detachment would know."

Before they even reached the cabin, they could hear voices. Male voices.

"Sounds like Rick's got company, sir."

"Sure does, Hogan. Wouldn't it be nice if it was the Grant brothers - but I don't feel that lucky today, do you?"

"No, sir." Actually, Hogan did feel that lucky. But it was better to agree with the boss. If it were the Grant brothers, he hoped they didn't start anything with their hunting rifles. Hogan had never used his gun yet. He kind of hoped to, someday. But not today.

Two men were seated on the doorstep of Rick Osmond's cabin. Each one had a mug in one hand and a cigarette in the other. There was a ski-doo parked near the trees on one side of the cabin.

"I'm Sergeant Jenkins of the RCMP. Are either of you Rick Osmond?" Jenkins doubted it even as he asked. Too old, too scruffy.

One of them spit out a mouthful of whatever liquid was in his mug and started laughing and wheezing; the other looked shocked.

"I'll take that as a no. Names, please?"

"I'm Mick Grant and he's Walter Grant. What can we do for you?"

"Is there anyone in that cabin?"

The two Grants looked at each other and smiled. Slyly.

"No."

"Mind if we all go in and have a chat?"

"Yes, we minds. But suit yourselves." The two men got up and went inside, and Jenkins and Hogan followed. Grandy sat down on the step to wait. Oh, for a smoke and a cup of whatever swill the Grants were drinking, no matter how bad it was.

The cabin was exactly the way Jenkins expected it to be. Dirty, with dilapidated furniture. He sat down on a rickety press-back wooden chair whose paint had seen better days. Hogan took a seat on another one exactly like it. His grandmother had chairs like this in her kitchen, but they had been carefully looked after, like the antiques they were.

"So, what are you boys doing in Rick Osmond's cabin?"

The one called Mick answered. "Because some bastard burnt ours. Besides, Rick don't need this cabin anymore."

"And why is that?"

"Because he's dead."

"Dead? What makes you think so?" Jenkins was feeling decidedly uneasy.

"Because his body is layin' in the shed out in back of this cabin."

Jenkins stood up. "Hogan handcuff these men and escort them to the chopper. I'm going to look in the shed. Give me a minute, and if I don't show up, come back."

Hogan knew what Jenkins was afraid of. That somehow

Rick Osmond was involved with the Grants, and that he wouldn't find a corpse in the shed at all, but a live man with a rifle. Or something like that. Things were getting tangly, as the locals said.

"Jesus, b'ys, we never done it!" Mick Grant looked as if he were being accused of stealing the communion wine.

"Yeah? We'll talk about that at the detachment."

His hand on his pistol, Jenkins walked the short distance to the decrepit shed behind the cabin. A lone crow flew squawking out of a tree behind the small structure, dislodging snow from a bough. One crow for sorrow, the saying went. And there would surely be sorrow inside that innocent structure. Sorrow for Osmonds' family, if the Grants were telling the truth. And if Osmond were in there alive, with a weapon, there would possibly be a lot more sorrow spread around. But it wasn't the first time Jenkins had been in this kind of situation. *Que sera.*

It took him a minute to adjust his eyes to the dim light after the brightness of the winter day outside. When he did, the most obvious object was a long blue tarp on the floor, covering something. Something the shape and size of a human body. He took out his gloves and put them on, and then pulled the tarp off one end of whatever it was hiding. And here was its secret: the remains of a human face. Jenkins gently covered it up again and went outside. He stood in the sun, looked at the green and white living trees and took a deep breath. And then he headed for the helicopter.

After a second helicopter with forensics arrived, and the sad process of dealing with a violent and possibly criminal death got underway, the first helicopter left and headed for Setback. Jenkins had the Grants deposited in an interview room. Later they would be dealt with separately, but for now, Jenkins wanted to observe them as a unit, all three of them. It might give him some clues as to how to proceed with them one-on-one.

"This is gettin' borin'," Bill said, the smart one. Jenkins wondered exactly how stupid his brothers must be, on a scale of one to ten. Two, three? Minus two or three?

"Maybe we could talk about what happened to that guy in the shed, whoever it is." Jenkins knew that last bit would get them talking.

"We told you – it's Rick Osmond."

"Well, that's yet to be established, but there is no reason to doubt you. What were you doing in Mr. Osmond's cabin?"

"We went up in the woods two days ago." This one was Mick, red hair, and bowlegs.

"You went to Osmond's cabin two days ago?"

"No, b'y, we went to our own cabin two days ago. But it wasn't there. Well, it was there, but it was flattened, burnt. Fucked. As you knows, we heard the chopper goin' over yesterday. Well, Walter heard it. I told him he was drunk and nuts. And he was, but then I heard it too."

"Who do you think did it?" Jenkins already had an idea about that. They'd burnt the cabin, then went to Rick Osmond's cabin, killed him, and were probably going to burn that cabin and the shed too. But why?

"We don't know. When we got to the cabin two mornin's ago, it was still smoulderin'."

"I knows who burnt it." This was Walter, the murderer. Wiry, dirty beard, close-set eyes. Jenkins' dog had more intelligence in its eyes than Walter did. More humanity, too.

"Who?"

"That cocksucker Rick Osmond."

"And why do you think Mr. Osmond would do that?"

"Well, there were three cabins: ours, Nagles', and Rick's. Two were burnt, and his wasn't. Do the math. You don't have to be a rocket scientist to figure it out."

No, thought Jenkins. But you'd have to be smarter than a turnip. And you aren't.

"Tell me about going to Mr. Osmond's cabin and finding the body."

"Well, it's a long story. We needs a cup of tea and some cigarettes first."

So, do I, thought Jenkins. Although he'd given up smoking three years ago.

The provisions were brought. After the brothers had a mouthful of tea and lit up a cigarette each, Jenkins spoke.

"So, tell me what happened."

Mick and Walter looked at Bill. He looked at each of them in turn and shrugged.

Mick spoke. "When we got to our cabin two days ago and found it burnt, we had a forty ouncer of rum with us. We had planned on drinkin' it while we were at the cabin for a few nights. After seein' what was left of the cabin, we drank the forty of rum right then and there. Out of the bottle. After the rum was gone, we were too drunk to take the ski-doo back to Setback, cause one of you lads might run us in. So, we went to Nagles' cabin to sober up. But when we got to Nagles' cabin, it was also burnt. So, we went to Rick's cabin."

Mick Grant stopped talking and lit another cigarette off the butt of the first one.

"Anyways, when we got inside Rick's place, there were three 40-ouncers of rum sittin' on the table. Let me correct that: there were two and a half 40-ouncers of rum, three dimes of weed, and a few grams of coke. So, we obliged ourselves, like ya would. Actually, we were drownin' our sorrows about the cabin.

Later on, the two of us passed out at the table. We never woke up 'til daylight. We mustered up some breakfast. Walter went to the bathroom for a shit– we'd been pissin' outside all night - and somethin' caught his eye on the way back through the open bedroom door - Rick's bedroom."

"I smelt somethin' first, Mick. A big Jesus stink." Walter looked like a prissy woman who had gotten wind of a fart.

Jenkins almost grinned. Walter had killed a man, hadn't he? Not his first sniff of a corpse.

"Right, Walter smelled somethin', and then he thought he saw somethin', so he went in the bedroom, and there was blood on the floor and there was Rick Osmond on the floor, dead as a doornail. We could see the hole between his two eyes. There was a handgun in his right hand, a big handgun. The type cowb'ys have in the movies, the ones that the cylinder can spin round. I don't know anythin' about handguns, I only know rifles and shotguns. I have a ten gauge single shot goose gun and a Lee Enfield .303, a relic from the war. I gets a moose or caribou with it every two or three years when I gets a set of tags. Anyways you should have heard Walter scream – it was pitched so high you'd have thought he had no nuts."

"You're sure he was dead? People sometimes survive being shot in the head."

Mick pursed his small mouth until it looked like a hen's arsehole. Not that Jenkins had ever seen a hen's arsehole, it was just an expression – "mouth like a hen's arsehole." His father used to use it sometimes, usually to describe a disagreeable old woman.

"Well, for one, officer, if he wasn't dead, don't you think he would have come out and had a few drinks with us? Especially it bein' his rum. And for two, when I touched him, he was ice cold."

"So, what did you do then?"

"We didn't know what to do, we were in a conundrum. Here we were in a man's cabin, and he was dead in it. And me brother here had already gone to jail for murder. You knows the story of Walter and Gerry Lyver, do you?"

"I do." Jenkins looked at Walter and wondered if he was going to be sent to a penitentiary on the mainland again. They only sent people who committed small crimes to the local penitentiary in St. John's. Any sentence over two years, and off you went to Springhill in Nova Scotia or Dorchester in New Brunswick. If Walter had killed Rick Osmond, he'd be facing a fairly long stretch of time.

"Okay, then you know why we figured we were in a fuckin' pickle, and I mean a big fuckin' pickle. We discussed it over a few more drinks. Why not? There was lots to drink and lots to discuss. After a few hours of discussin' it, we decided we'd better lay the poor bastard out in the shed. We figured it would be safe out there in the cold. Be like a primitive morgue."

"Why did you decide to place the body in the shed?" Besides the fact, you were dead drunk, and any idea comes tied up in red ribbons when you're in that state. Jenkins had had a few of those ideas himself back in his younger days.

"Well, for a number of reasons. Well, he was dead, wasn't he? We couldn't leave him in the cabin. You could bend anchors with the heat in the cabin. It was only a matter of time before he smelled worse than he did. Second, we had some drinkin' left to do. So, we laid him out in the shed in the cold.

He wasn't goin' anywhere. We figured we'd tell you cowb'ys what we found once we finished the rum and got back home."

"Any idea who killed him?" Ah – that had them rattled. The three of them crossed their arms almost in unison and scowled. It made them look even more like the troll in the book of fairy tales Jenkins' mother used to read to him when he was little. He was getting tired just from being around such low, sucking energy.

"Haven't got a fuckin' clue. Not Walter and me, that's for fuckin' sure."

"What about you, Bill? You've been very quiet. Did you kill Rick Osmond?"

Bill Grant uncrossed his arms and sat back in his chair. He smiled at Jenkins. "No, I never killed him. He was nothin' to me, but a prick, and I haven't been in the back-country in a week. And didn't Mick just tell you, there was a hole between the two eyes with a gun in his hand? If that's not suicide, I don't know what is."

The prick? Jenkins would talk to Bill Grant later. He'd be talking to all of them a lot more than he wanted to before this case was solved if it ever was. Despite what the public thought, the Mounties didn't always get their man.

"Walter, Mick - tell me about moving the body to the shed. Take your time – I want all the details."

Mick again. Maybe he didn't have anyone to talk to, and this was his big chance.

"Well, we were loaded drunk. We rolled him in a bunch of

blankets and then we wondered if a tarp or somethin' was layin' around, and yes there was – a big blue one out in the shed. So, then we rolled him, along with the gun, in that and tied it with some twine we also found out there. And then we lugged him out. He was a fine lug. Now I knows what they means about dead weight. Walter already knew, didn't you Walter?"

Walter looked straight ahead as Mick winked and nudged him with his elbow. Jenkins figured Mick would be sporting a black eye on account of that remark to his brother as soon as they got out. If they got out.

"You weren't worried a weasel, or a mink may have gotten in the shed and fed on the body?"

"We didn't really give a fuck. Listen, we didn't like Rick Osmond and he never liked me or me brothers. So, we didn't give a fuck what happened to his smelly corpse."

After they were taken back to the cells, Jenkins went out and stood in the cold night air. The stars were as finely etched as snowflakes and as plentiful. He allowed himself five minutes of peace and an imaginary cigarette, and then went back inside the detachment.

"Well, Hogan, we now have two murders and no murderer."

"Yes, sir. Um . . . no, sir. Did you get anything from the Grants?" Hogan had been glad when Jenkins told him he'd rather interview the three brothers by himself. They'd reminded him of stories his grandmother used to tell him.

Scary stories used to send him right under the bedclothes. But there was always a night light on when he came back out. And Gran never minded if he climbed in bed with her when he couldn't settle down. But sometimes when he'd thought he'd like to get in her bed, he'd wonder if she'd turn into the big, bad wolf like the grandmother in the other story. Those old tales sure did a good job of scaring children. He'd never let his future kids near them. The idea of one of your closest relatives turning out to be a monster – as if that ever happened in real life.

Chapter 22

"Dr. Delmont, this is Sergeant Jenkins. I'd like to see you as soon as possible. Are you available right now?"

The Sergeant's voice was tight as a corset. Delmont had worn one once, in a school play. She hadn't enjoyed it, and she wasn't enjoying the sound of Jenkins' voice. Something was up, and it wasn't a good something.

"Yes. I don't have another appointment until this afternoon. You can come by the office now if it's convenient."

"Actually, it might not be convenient. Is Sally Osmond at work today?"

Sally? Delmont felt an unpleasant sensation in her gut. "Yes, she is. Why?'

"I'll tell you that when I see you. Can you come out to the detachment without letting Ms. Osmond know?"

"Sure. I'll be right over."

Another grey day, with a moaning wind. Delmont pulled up her collar for the short but chilly walk to the RCMP detachment at the rear of the building. Had something happened to Sally's parents? Or Rick? She was about to find out.

Twenty minutes later Delmont and Jenkins took the same short but chilly walk together on their way to Sally's office. Sally would be devastated by what Jenkins was about to tell her. She was pretty shaken up herself. Another dead man, Rick Osmond this time. Jenkins hadn't given her any details, but then she hadn't expected him to.

Jenkins knocked on Sally's door, and Delmont winced as she heard the cheerful. "Come in!"

The girl looked puzzled when she saw the RCMP officer. She looked at Delmont as though she were seeking some explanation of his presence. Whatever she saw in Delmont's face didn't reassure her.

"What is it, Sergeant? What's wrong? It's not mom or dad, is it?"

"No, Ms. Osmond. May Dr. Delmont and I sit down?"

"Oh my gosh, yes. You don't need to ask." Sally's face suddenly changed as a thought hit home.

"It's Rick, isn't it, Sergeant. I knew he was goin' to cause trouble when you talked to him, but he doesn't mean to be so — so saucy, he really don't. Oh, my God, did you arrest Rick? Mom and Dad will have —"

Jenkins rubbed a hand across his forehead and then abruptly interrupted Sally's sentence. "Ms. Osmond. I'm sorry to have to tell you this, but your brother, Rick, is dead."

Sally looked at Jenkins with an open mouth, putting both her hands in the air, palms facing him, as though she were trying to shove him away. Trying to shove away what he'd just said, which hung on the air like the crack of doom. Delmont got up and went to her, but the girl shrank away. Her voice, when it finally emerged, was barely audible.

"What happened to him?"

"We don't know yet, Ms. Osmond. It was a gunshot wound. We need a family member to travel to St. John's and identify him for us. We can take you or your parents there if you don't want to drive."

"I can't . . . can't. Where did he die?" At least shock was keeping Sally from being hysterical, thought Delmont. The tears and screams would come later.

"At his cabin."

Delmont looked at Jenkins, who nodded at her imperceptibly.

"Sally let me take you home now. I'll stay with you until you feel you can cope on your own. Sergeant Jenkins is going to talk to your parents now."

Sally got to her feet. "I'm goin' with him. I'm not lettin' mom and dad face this by themselves. Oh my God, this will kill them!" Delmont caught Sally as her legs buckled and the keening began. The noise was inhuman, as it often was when life dealt a nearly mortal blow. Delmont remembered a patient who had woken up to find her baby dead in his crib of SIDS. The cries that had come out of her when she told Delmont about it had raised the small hairs on her neck.

"Sally, I'll call your minister and let him know what's happened. I know your parents will want to talk with him. And I can let your Doctor know, as well, in case you think he might need to drop by and give you and your parents a prescription for sedatives. Whatever I can do, Sally, I will do. I'm only a phone call away, here or at home. I'm so sorry, Sally – you don't deserve to have to go through this. No one does."

Sergeant Jenkins took Sally by the arm and guided her out the door. Delmont sat back down. She needed to collect her thoughts before she went back to her office. The first thing she needed to do was cancel her appointments for the rest of the day. She needed to be free in case Sally called. Delmont shuddered as she thought of the scene being or about to be played out at Sally's parents' house. Their only son, and her mother's "baby." Perhaps Rick would still be alive if he hadn't been babied, but you never knew, really, although there was a lot of literature on the subject. The good old Oedipal complex. But what had happened to Rick? Had he known something about Terry Ross's death that had made him the target of the killer? Delmont felt a sudden craving for a drink. Possibly two or three.

When Jenkins got back from the Osmond residence, there was a message on the answering machine. It was from the Anglican Minister asking for an officer to call him immediately. Jenkins dialed the number and introduced himself. "Good day officer, I have something in my possession that you will want to read. A week ago, Rick Osmond dropped by my residence and gave me a sealed envelope. He asked me not to open it and to pass it along to the authorities if he never came back for it in a few weeks. I will say, young Osmond was distraught and was somewhat intoxicated when he was here. You can drop by and pick up this envelope. I'll be home all day."

"Thank you for calling. I'll be there in five minutes."

This call was unexpected. As Jenkins drove to the Minister's residence, he wondered what Rick Osmond had written that was important and confidential enough to give to his Minister.

When Jenkins got back to the detachment, he poured a coffee, and sat at his desk, he put on rubber gloves and gently opened the envelope with an envelope opener.

"Go talk to Rock McGee. The answers you are looking for are under lock and key. Rick."

Jenkins was shocked and dumbfounded by what he had just read. He radioed Hogan and asked to attend at the detachment immediately. He passed the letter to Hogan when he walked in.

Hogan spoke and said, "This is interesting. I suspect we're going to Longview?"

"Yes, immediately."

When they walked into Longview, McGee and a short, red-haired girl were shooting pool. Jenkins walked up to McGee and said, "We need to speak to you alone, now!"

"Sure, not a problem, follow me."

When they were in McGee's office, Jenkins said, "We've come across a note written by Rick Osmond. In this note, it says talk to Rock McGee, the answers you are looking for are under lock and key."

"What? Why talk to me? I know of no answers under lock and key!"

"Rock, why would Osmond say somethin' like this in a note."

"Officer, I have no idea why he said such a thing."

Jenkins was about to speak, McGee interrupted him. "I, I might have what you're lookin' for."

"What?"

"I may know what you're lookin' for and where it is. A couple of days after Ross was killed, I called Rick and asked him could he jimmi up somethin' to secure the lid to the flush box, in the men's washroom. I've had three broken in half in the past year or so. Rick was handy, at woodworkin' and a decent welder. He came in and measured up the flush box and came back later with flat iron straps, he made up two braces to secure the top on the flush box. He secured them with a lock at the bottom of the box. He even bought a lock and gave one key to it. I was surprised he only gave me one key, as locks come with two keys. I guess he kept the second key, but why? We may now know why. Let me get the key from behind the bar."

All three walked into the washroom. The officers could see the one-inch iron straps on the flush box. McGee bent down and unlocked the lock at the bottom of the flush box and removed the straps. He lifted the lid and turned it over. Attached to the inside of the lid was duct tape, hiding something. McGee held the lid out to Jenkins. Jenkins hauled on a pair of gloves and removed the tape and could see a small white envelope inside a plastic baggy. He took the baggy and tape. He thanked McGee for his quick thinking.

When the officers got back to the detachment both poured a coffee. Jenkins hauled on a pair of rubber gloves and removed the envelope from the baggy, he opened the envelope with an envelope opener.

"Mom, Dad, Sally, Bette. If you're reading this, I am gone. I had no choice. I killed Terry Ross, and I can't go to prison. There's 5,000 dollars plus in my bank account. Sell my cabin, truck, boat and motor and bike and put what you get for that in an account for Bette's education. Bette be a good girl for your mom. Stay in school, stay away from drugs and booze and losers like me. I love you, Bette, and I always will. Mom, Dad, Sally I'm so sorry. I hate to hurt you like this, but it's the only way out. See you on the other side. All my Love, Rick."

Jenkins passed the letter to Hogan when he finished reading it. After Hogan finished reading the letter. Jenkins spoke, "This answers so many questions."

Hogan replied, "It answers all our questions. We now know who killed Ross and Osmond's death was a suicide. Technically, our job is done."

The weapon found with Rick Osmond's body was a .38 Special, standard issue for the RCMP. The serial number confirmed it was Terry Ross's service revolver. Two bullets were missing from the cylinder, this weapon holds six bullets. Telling investigators that the bullet that kill Osmond was most likely from Ross's service revolver. Results from the Halifax Crime Lab confirmed that Ross was killed with a bullet from a .38 Special.

Three hours later, there was a knock on Delmont's door. A soft knock. She had just gotten out of the bath and was on her second drink of Vermouth, which she intended to finish in bed. A short nap on a day like this would give her the strength she needed in case Sally got in touch with her later. Delmont knew she was suffering from mild shock herself. Setback had been slowly chipping away at her robust mental health, and the two murders hadn't helped any. Perhaps she should take a week off, fly back home? Not now, but perhaps when the dust settled a bit for Sally and her family.

The knock sounded again, more insistent this time. A small frisson of fear slid up Delmont's back. Which local was on the other side of her front door this time? Well, whoever it was, she was not at home to them. She put on a ragged pair of sweatpants and a paint-stained T-shirt and wrapped her wet hair in a towel. And then she heard Jenkins' voice, as loud and clear as if he were standing in the living room instead of on her front steps.

"Dr. Delmont, I'd really like to speak with you if you're in there. Please."

Jesus in a tutu, what now? She'd have to answer the door because if she didn't, he'd be back again, no doubt.

"Sorry, Sergeant, I was in the bath. Obviously." She tugged on the towel covering her hair.

"It's Benedick – Ben."

"Benedick? Unusual choice. Unless you're Shakespeare."

Jenkins grinned. It made him look ten years younger, thought Delmont. And almost handsome.

"Yeah, well, my mother loved that play, *Much Ado About Nothing*. She was the first – and last – member of her family to go to university. Not that it did her much good. She ended up as a housekeeper and a baby producer just like most women of her time."

The grin disappeared as quickly as it had appeared. "Dr. Delmont -"

"It's Patricia. Patricia Beatrice. Tish"

The grin was back again. "Well, that's quite a coincidence. Benedick and Beatrice, just like in Shakespeare's play. They weren't that fond of each other, though, were they."

It was Delmont's turn to grin. Not at first. He was a pill,

and she had to put him in his place. And then they liked each other very much. "Please, come in and sit down. I was just about to light a fire. Want some coffee?"

"I could use a cup of coffee. Two cream, no sugar, please."

Delmont made the coffee and put some chocolate biscuits on an old English plate she'd found in one of the cupboards. She put the cups and the plate on an old black tin tray with roses on it, courtesy of the same cupboard. When she brought the tray into the living room, Jenkins was staring into the fire as if he were lost in a dream.

"Fire giving you any clues?"

Jenkins started, and then laughed – quick and sardonic, it was. "No, not really. Forensics is still at work on the site of Osmond's death. The exhibits guy is there too. What would be nice would be some DNA evidence unequivocally solving both deaths, Osmond's, and Ross's, but this isn't a fairytale."

"Oh, I don't know. Setback is strange enough to qualify for a fairytale ending to one of its stories – a Grimm's fairytale ending anyway."

"Ah, the Grimm brothers. My mother used to read those to me. The worst one was the little girl in the red shoes, who couldn't stop dancing until they cut off her feet. She was being punished for being vain, for liking coloured shoes, if I remember correctly."

"Yes, she was. Only it was Hans Christian Andersen, not the Grimms. Hard to tell them apart, really. Those old folktales, they were brutal. Kept people in line, though, which was one of their purposes. All mythology does that, or tries to, including Christian mythology. But I don't suppose you came here to discuss any of that, did you?"

She was so small. He hadn't noticed that before. She was one of those people whose personality or strength of character makes them seem taller. Small, but perfectly made. The curve of her jaw and her long, white neck under the towel turban made him want to reach out and touch her face.

Jenkins cleared his throat. "No, I didn't. Some other time, maybe. Dr. – Tish, I'm here because the last time I talked to you, I got the distinct impression you were withholding information about Rick Osmond. Were you?"

A blush coloured Delmont's cheeks, making her even more desirable. Jenkins hoped he would be able to leave this house without doing anything he'd regret later, but if she made one move, the smallest little move . . . he sighed and waited.

"Guilty as charged, Sergeant – Ben. I didn't think it had any relevance to your inquiry."

Oh, what a perfect stubborn mouth she had. He could definitely kiss it more than once if he had to. "But you know you're required to tell officers investigating a serious crime anything you are told in confidence if it relates to the crime."

Delmont's back was as stiff as a poker, and her lovely chin was in the air. "But it was not told to me in *professional* confidence. And I fully believed it didn't relate to Terry Ross's murder. But if Rick has been murdered too . . .. The thing is, I don't want this to get out – it would destroy Sally and her family."

"As you know, the RCMP doesn't gratuitously spread gossip around. Not that some of us aren't guilty of that sometimes, being human beings and all, but I assure you that whatever you tell me will be held in the strictest confidence unless there's a court case and it absolutely has to come out. Okay?"

"Okay." Delmont leaned towards him, just slightly. Just enough for him to notice she wasn't wearing a bra under her T-shirt. Oh God, he should have brought Hogan with him, but he hadn't. He'd been afraid she wouldn't talk if she felt ganged up on.

Delmont saw his downward glance. She smiled internally. The feeling in her chest that had begun shortly after he'd come in intensified. They said the Mounties always got their man. Well, so did she.

"Rick Osmond had sex with Terry Ross, possibly more than once. And he was furious at Ross for it. Said he was a devil, making him do something like that. The boy was either a closet homosexual or somewhere in the middle of the sexual spectrum. Whatever he was, he knew that life in Setback would come to an end for him if what he did with Ross ever got out. Which is funny really – some of the men I've met in Setback seem to be emotional homosexuals, considering the way they treat women and how they hang out with one another almost exclusively."

Jesus H. Christ. Ross had been gay? Osmond too? Jenkin's mind started to prick up its ears like a pointer on the scent of a partridge. "Tish, I appreciate the information. And I'm not going to scold you for not telling me earlier."

Delmont smiled like the proverbial cat that had swallowed the canary. "Oh well, Ben, I don't mind a little scolding now and then. Depending on who's doing it." She stood up and moved to stand beside his chair. And then she reached out and put her hand on his chest.

Jenkins groaned and pulled her down on his lap. He'd known he was doomed from the moment he'd walked in. But what a glorious doom it was!

"Okay, Hogan, we're going to go talk to the Grant brothers one more time, and then we'll let them go."

"Yes, sir. Excuse me for asking, sir, but did you just get some good news? About the case?"

Hogan had obviously picked up on Jenkins' post-coital mood. But he'd never guess. Jenkins found it hard to believe himself. She had been a genius in bed, a true genius. As if she'd known all about what made him tick. Maybe it was because she was a psychologist. If that were the case, he'd have to remember to date more of them. "No, Hogan, nothing's come back from forensics yet, of course. Too early."

He wasn't going to share what Tish Delmont had told him with anyone unless he had to.

The Grants were starting to smell even worse than they did previously. Time to let them go home and shower if they ever did.

"Well, Messieurs Grant, if you have anything to add to what you told us yesterday, feel free. Otherwise, you can leave."

Chapter 23

"It's the Grants, them goddamn Grants, I know it is."
Delmont kept her eyes on the road, but she felt like turning her
head and yelling "Shut up!" at Sally. It had been a rough day.
She'd offered to drive Sally to St. John's to identify Rick's
body, and the girl had taken her up on it. Sally had sobbed
nearly the whole way to the city, but the shock of seeing Rick
on that white metal table in the morgue had quietened her
down. She was starting up again, however, and they still had
many kilometres to go. Delmont was tempted to ask her to
take the wheel, but she didn't trust Sally's driving given the
emotional state she was in. Delmont wasn't feeling too steady
herself. The dead white face with the bullet hole between the
eyes kept superimposing itself between her view of the
highway and the barren scenery. Poor, poor boy. If he had

been brought up somewhere else, he might be alive right now. Delmont cursed the demon ignorance under her breath.

Apparently, Sally thought Delmont was cursing her. "I'm sorry, Tish, I really am, but I hates the fact that the Grant brothers are out there walkin' around while Rick is lyin' there . . . oh, Rick."

Well, at least Sally was weeping silently now. She'd probably doze off soon, poor thing. Exhaustion is a friend, sometimes.

But Sally wasn't ready for sleep yet. "Tish, poor mother hasn't been out of the bed since she heard Rick was dead. She dropped like a stone when we told her. Dad had to pick her up and take her to the bedroom. And she won't eat nothin' but a bit of soup or tea every now and again – oh Tish, what will I do if mom dies too?"

"Sally! You need to get yourself together. You won't be any good to either of your parents if you don't. Also, I'm trying to get us back to Setback safely, and that's getting harder to accomplish with someone as overtly upset as you are beside me. I'm not made of stone, you know. Why don't you try to sleep a little?"

Like a large, obedient child, Sally let her head fall against the back of the seat and closed her eyes. Her hand crept out until it found the hem of Delmont's coat, and her fingers closed around it. Delmont half expected the thumb on the other hand to disappear into her mouth, but it found its way into Sally's coat pocket with its fellow fingers instead. Poor, poor Sally. Delmont reached out and stroked the dark, silky hair. It felt so different from Ben Jenkin's stiff, thick blonde-grey thatch. She felt herself relax. She'd have to entice him back again, although she didn't think he'd need much enticing. A quick phone call would do.

"Rock McGee's here, sir."

Hogan looked like he'd just handed Jenkins a present. And maybe he had. McGee had hired himself a lawyer, who had just called Jenkins about McGee's coming in to talk to them about Rick Osmond. She wanted the assault charges against McGee dropped in exchange for the information her client had to offer. What McGee had to tell them was worth it, she said. Also, she wanted Jenkins to assure her that he wouldn't press charges based on anything McGee said to incriminate himself. Jenkins agreed. Unless it involved babies and Satanic rituals. She hung up on him. No sense of humour.

McGee sat in the interview room looking like a bull wearing a leather jacket. His head dropped when the officers entered. He looked for all the world as if he was going to charge, thought Jenkins. One of his feet was pawing the floor under the table.

"Cigarette, Mr. McGee?"

"No thanks. It's bad for the wind. I works out. Don't mind if I take off my jacket. It's warm here." McGee flexed his back and arms. Jenkins thought to himself that it was a bit pointless of the man not to smoke when he worked in what was essentially a smokehouse.

"So, Mr. McGee, why are you here today?"

"I got a few things to tell you about Rick." McGee glanced at his lawyer, who nodded.

"Rick Osmond was sellin' drugs in Setback and up and down the coast. Rick sold everythin' - weed, hash, acid, coke and St. Pierre and Miquelon booze. He started sellin' about four months ago. And he told me that Ross was tryin' to be a super cop and was on him like a bloodhound on a scent. Watchin' him every time he moved. Searchin' his truck whenever he felt like it. When I beat up Ross, Rick told me I did the right thing. He said I should have killed him."

Jenkins exchanged glances with Hogan. There had been no record of any of this in Ross's files. There had been no mention of Rick Osmond anywhere in the files. Thanks to Delmont, Jenkins knew why that was. But to let a major drug dealer off the hook – sex wasn't worth a man's whole career. Because sooner or later Osmond would have been caught by someone else, and Ross would have been hauled up on the carpet over it. Maybe Ross just hadn't had enough to go on. After all, McGee seemed to think that Osmond had only been dealing for four months.

"Mr. McGee, where was Rick Osmond getting his drugs?"

Again, the nod from the lawyer. "A fella from Lewisporte was his supplier. They had a great setup. Rick's dealer came here in a speed boat once a week - always a weekday, always after dark and a good weather day."

"Where would they meet?"

"They wouldn't. Rick was smarter than that. They had a grapnel tied off five or six hundred feet from the bottom of Dead Man's Gulch. They had a rope looped into an eye-ring on a grapnel and tied into an eye-ring onshore, tied to a large rock, with a cable. There was a two-gallon gas can attached to this rope, the gas can was painted a flat grey, not to be noticed by fishermen. The dealer put the drugs in it, Rick would leave the money he owed him in it after he sold the drugs. You can stuff a lot of weed and hash and stuff in a two-gallon gas can. They had weight in the bottom of the gas can so it would stay under the water, so fishermen wouldn't spot it. And they always hauled up their money or drugs after dark."

"Mr. McGee, do you know how this dealer got in touch with Rick? I doubt Rick encouraged him to call him at his parents' house."

This time McGee looked long and hard at his lawyer. She put her hand on his arm and squeezed it and nodded once again. "He would call the payphone at the club on an even hour – two, four or six o'clock - and hang up in my face two times in a row. That was a message for me to tell Rick his drugs were ready for pickup. I'd call Rick at his house. If he wasn't there, I'd leave a message for him to call me. When he got the message, he'd come to the club, and I'd tell him what time his call came in. The call was usually made within eighteen hours after the drop-off."

"What if you didn't answer the phone?"

"Well, that wasn't a problem. As soon as the phone rang, I'd look at my watch and watch it like a hawk. So, whoever answered it, and it was the drug call, would answer it twice in less than thirty seconds. So, even if I never made it to the phone, I knew it was the drug call."

"Why were you involved with this Mr. McGee?"

McGee crossed his arms and stared at the table. His lawyer looked at Jenkins and rolled her eyes. Jenkins' shrugged. "Mr. McGee, I have assured Ms. Green here that unless you killed Ross or Osmond, we have no interest whatsoever in your activities."

McGee looked up and scowled. His muscle bound tattooed arms were still crossed. "I was sellin' drugs for Rick - on a small scale - out of the club. So, he asked me to take the call for him at the club. I had no problem with it – sure, it's a public payphone, you can't stop anyone from callin' it."

"So, there's an eye-ring and line at the bottom of Dead Man's Gulch?"

"I doubt it."

"Why?"

"Well, don't you think the dealer from Lewisporte was

stupid enough to leave it there? I'd say within hours of hearin' of Rick's death, he took the grapnel and line out of it. You might find the eye-ring on the shoreline."

"You seem confident of that."

"Well, officers, do the math. I'm sure there's a chance the dealer figured Rick may have told someone about the setup. I'm sure it's gone. It would be worth your while to search for the eye-ring I suppose." McGee grinned and dropped his arms.

"Do you know the name of the dealer from Lewisporte?" Jenkins knew this was a long shot: McGee wouldn't want to get himself in trouble with a major drug dealer.

"I used to know it, but for some reason, I have forgotten it," McGee said with an evil grin.

"I see. Anything else you would like to tell us, Rick Osmond?"

The lawyer inclined her head and McGee took a deep breath. "Yeah. Rick slashed the tires on Ross's jeep."

"How do you know that?"

"He told me. Rick hated Ross for the houndin' he was givin' him. And he also hated him for hangin' around his sister. You know what we calls women who go out with cops around here? We call them copsuckers."

McGee's hyena laugh sounded odd coming out of a bull. Jenkins had had about enough of looking at and listening to McGee. "Anything else?"

McGee looked sullen. "No, nothin'. I feels bad for Rick's family. His sister and mother will never get over this – Mrs.

thought the sun shone out of Rick's arsehole. I'm goin' to miss him myself. A little wild when he was on the booze and drugs, but, overall, a fine fella. That's three buddies of mine gone since the cod moratorium. All self-destructed. I have this philosophy, some people you can take to all the Psychologists and Psychiatrists in the world and try all the different types of antidepressant and antipsychotic medications on them, but when they make up their minds there's nothin' we can do. The burden one man carries, another man cannot carry that same burden. For some people, this is the only way out and their only answer. Always remember we're here for a good time, not a long time. And by the way, Sergeant – as much as I despise you guys, we need you. The world would be a sad and dangerous place without police in it."

Jenkins hid his surprise and his smile. McGee the philosopher, who'd a thunk it?

"Okay, Mr. McGee, you can go." And if you do one thing out of line from here on in, we'll come down on you like a ton of bricks. Jenkins was sure McGee would be back at the detachment in the not-so-distant future. That's about all the future held for men like him.

Osmond's cause of death was not released to the public up to now. Jenkin's never questioned Rock on why he thought Rick Osmond had taken his own life. He knew well enough, that finding the suicide note at Longview was enough to tell MeGee this.

The next morning Campbell and the fire chief rappelled down over the cliff into Dead Man's Gulch and sure enough, they found the eye-ring attached to a large boulder with cable. It was roughly three hundred feet from where the RCMP cruiser had landed when it was pushed over the cliff. This gave a lot of credibility to what McGee had said.

Jenkins was looking at the two notes Rick Osmond had written. He picked up the piece of paper and put it in his attaché case. He'd have to speak with Tish Delmont and Sally Osmond immediately. He was not looking forward to it. Perhaps he could get in closer touch – the closest touch - with Tish afterwards if that were possible. From the look on her face when he'd kissed her goodbye the other day, it surely was. Jenkins sighed, and then got up and put his coat and boots on.

Delmont tried to ignore the knock on her office door, but she knew it was futile. Everyone knew she was at work: her car was in the parking lot. It wasn't Sally. The girl would knock and then enter if she knew Delmont was alone. And she'd told Sally earlier that she had no patients to see until later in the afternoon. So, who was it?

"Come in." She watched as the door opened slowly. Oh, Jesus in a flannel petticoat, it wasn't Bill Grant, was it? The big bad wolf in RCMP clothing. No, he was in plainclothes, as usual, but cops in plainclothes looked like cops anyway, the same way their unmarked vehicles looked like cop cars.

"Hello."

He looked as nervous as a cat. Uncertain. Good. She'd keep him that way for a little while, and then she'd kiss him silly.

"Hey. Ben." She hoped she sounded cool as a cucumber, although she didn't feel that way. Could he tell?

Jenkins felt relief course through his body. Although her face was impassive, he could feel the emotions flowing through her – the same ones that were flowing through him. He wanted to burst out laughing, but that would only get her back up. He thought of the arch of her back over him in the bed and sternly told his mind that there were a lot of sad things to get through first.

She suddenly smiled at him. "Business or pleasure?"

The last word curled around Jenkins like the tail of a sensual cat. He shook his head. "Business. First, anyway. And a sad business it is. Read this." He sat down in the chair in front of her desk, took the notes out of his case and pushed them across the wooden surface.

Delmont's hands were shaking. Ben reached across the desk and took one of them in his. "Tish -"

Suddenly she was in his lap for a second time, crying her heart out. "Oh, Ben, Ben – this is all my fault! If I had only told you at the beginning what Rick told me, we could have saved him. My God, I can't believe I didn't pick up on how sick he was. Oh, Christ, I think I'm going to throw up."

Tish called Sally at Jenkin's request. Half an hour later, a white-faced Delmont and a grim-faced Jenkins were sitting in Sally Osmond's office.

"Sally, there's a few things I have to discuss with you. After I left your parents' house the morning Rick's body was found, I had a few stops, I never got back to the detachment for a few hours. When I got back there was a message on the answering machine from your Minister. I suspect he left it after he left your parents' residence. He wanted to speak to an officer immediately. I called back and attended his residence shortly thereafter. He gave me an envelope that Rick had given him some days before. Rick had told the Minister if he never came back for it in a few weeks to give it to the authorities. When I opened the envelope, it said. "Talk to Rock McGee – the answers are under lock and key." When I read this, I was dumbfounded. Hogan and I went directly to Longview and spoke with McGee. At first, he never had a clue what we were looking for. Then it hit him. A few days after Ross was found, McGee had Rick in to construct some type of secure device to hold to the lid of the flush box in the men's washroom. When we removed the cover, we found an envelope attached to the cover with a note in it written by Rick. Here are both notes. Please take your time reading these."

Sally read both notes. She stared at the writing, unable to

speak. Tears freely flowed down her cheeks. Tish passed the tissues she took from her purse.

After a few minutes, she finally spoke. "This will devastate Mom and Dad, we know Rick had issues and faults. But havin' raised a son who is a murderer, not only a murderer but a murderer of a police officer."

Chapter 24

Jenkins was getting ready to go somewhere he didn't want to go - Rick Osmond's wake at the funeral home. Osmond had been cremated in St. John's and his ashes sent home to Setback. Rick was the first person in the community to have been cremated. Cremation was unusual in Setback, but so had the trajectory of the boy's life been. Poor, unstable kid. Tish had told him that Sally's mother had recently told her that her mother and an uncle had been alcoholics who had self-destructed. Sally seemed to put it down to their Mi'kmaq blood and was using that to have something to hang Rick's tragedy on, but Jenkins knew that it was impossible to know what was in a man's – or a woman's, for that matter – head or heart when they took a life, their own or another's. What path or paths led precisely to that moment was anyone's guess. There was usually great pain of some kind involved, Jenkins knew that much unless he or she was a sociopath or a psychopath. And Rick Osmond had not been one of those.

Terry Ross had been culpable in his own death, but Jenkins had left that out of the report. The drug dealing was enough of a motive. Neither Ross's nor Osmond's family needed to suffer on the score of their sons' homosexuality, especially since neither of the families had been told about it by those sons. The dead and the living deserved whatever honour could be pulled up out of their short lives.

Jenkins felt obligated to attend the official wake, to show that the RCMP felt no ill will towards the family, and because of Sally Osmond's face when she had read the suicide note. It would be good to get back to St. John's. Perhaps he could talk Tish into coming with him. She needed to get out of Setback for a while. Hell, what they both needed was to get off the island, but he wasn't due any leave for several months, and she had to finish her contract. In the meantime, though, perhaps they could have a few days or a week in the capital city. He could take her around to all the landmarks and museums and good restaurants, take her mind off what had happened. And there were other ways to distract her if he remembered correctly. He smiled then, for the first time that day.

It was one of those Newfoundland days that ran from early spring back to winter and then back to spring in the space of hours. Delmont had been at the graveside, at Sally's request. The wind had been blowing across a scowling sky like a banshee, but by the time the ceremony was over, the banshee had fled, and the sun was out and smiling like a Newfoundland grandmother. For days, Delmont doubted she'd ever smile again, but this morning as they were leaving the funeral home, Ben Jenkins had slipped a note into her coat pocket. This time next week, she'd be in St. John's.

In the meantime, she was here at the unofficial, traditional Newfoundland wake in the home – and the garage – of Sally's parents. Accordions and violins – fiddles – and lots of food and booze. And dancing. They seemed to be dancing poor Rick into the dark – or perhaps out of it? Most of the community had turned up, despite the family shame of having a son who had killed a man, and a police officer to boot, and then himself. Delmont felt sad for Sally and her parents. They certainly didn't deserve to be punished for what their son had done. Rick didn't deserve punishment either. Delmont was generally an agnostic, but in her heart of hearts, she hoped there was redemption somewhere, sometime. Not just for people like Rick, but for all humans, those queer animals who had to navigate a vicious world where everything alive fed off something else living, and who were the only beings conscious enough to see the tragedy of that. Some days she wondered why the whole race hadn't just collectively jumped over a cliff. But then she put her hand in her coat pocket and remembered why.

Sally came and put her arm in Delmont's. "Tish, did you get somethin' to eat? Mom made the cherry cake, you got to have a piece of that. And you got nothin' to drink, let me go get –"

Delmont held Sally's arm in a firm grip. "I had some of that cherry cake, Sally – and, as you say, it's deadly. And I had a cup of coffee. Don't really want anything stronger, and I'm driving, after all. How are you doing?"

The girl's face began to tighten up, the new lines became prominent, but suddenly, it relaxed. "I'm okay, Tish, I really am. Rick wouldn't want me to be sad. I know he's at peace, I can feel it in my soul. And Mom and Dad are feelin' better, with all the people here. They never expected all of them to come out, that's for sure, but they did." A tear trickled down one cheek and was wiped away.

"Of course, they did, Sally. Look, they all knew Rick, knew him ever since he was a kid, and they know that whatever was going on with him he wasn't a cold-blooded killer, just a tormented boy. And they all think the world of you and your parents, you know that, so why wouldn't they come? And like them, I'm honoured to be here."

Sally kissed Delmont on the cheek. And then she sighed. "Thanks for sayin' that, Tish. And I know you well enough to know you meant it, too. I'll miss you when you're gone, and it won't be long now."

The airport was fogged in; no planes were coming or going. This was standard in St. John's, the foggiest city in Canada. Especially in the spring. St. John's was also the cloudiest, snowiest, and windiest city in the country according to some sources. But it was beautiful today at twilight, even if Delmont was navigating a pea-soup fog that made her think of Jack the Ripper. She was going to meet Ben at a pub on Water Street; a small Irish pub that would be uninhabited at this hour. She was supposed to be on a plane to Chicago right now, but the lovely fog – blessed fog! – had grounded her, and so she would see Ben one more time, at least.

And there he was, looming up out of the fog, coming to meet her. She was in front of Erin's Pub now.

"Hello, Jack. Fancy meeting you here."

"Jack?" He took her hand, and they entered the warm pub that stank of beer and stale smoke. A thin man with a beard and a wide smile was wiping the bar, the same guy who'd been on duty the night before. Delmont thought the place looked like a movie set, but what movie it was set for, she couldn't say. Maybe one about a woman from another country who gets mixed up in a crime but then finds true love. She smiled to herself.

Jenkins looked at her quizzically.

"Sorry, Ben. Jack as in Jack the Ripper – you kind of came out of the fog like him. And why am I laughing? I don't know. Maybe the fog is making me crazy, or I picked up a crazy bug in Setback."

"Ah, Setback. There's no end of crazy out there. But I guess it helps to be crazy if you have to live in a crazy climate on top of a rock. Have you heard from Sally Osmond lately?"

"Yes, I was talking to her last night. It seems she has a serious beau these days, Jimmy Parsons. I met him – he won't let her down, I don't think." She made a face. "But what do I know? I was dead wrong about her brother."

"Let me get the beer, Tish, and then we'll talk about that."

She watched him walk to the bar and come back with a couple of pints of Guinness. He looked so good, like a man who knew who he was – and maybe who she was too. Delmont drew back from the latter thought: she knew who she was, and that was enough. But it was good to be with someone who really saw you, all the same. Someone who looked and listened, someone intelligent to his core. Too bad that this was probably their last night.

"Why so glum, lady?"

"Oh, you know. Parting is such sweet sorrow, and all that."

"Just can't leave Shakespeare out of it, can you?"

"No, Benedick, it seems I can't."

"Anyway, it wasn't your fault about Rick. I've been a cop for twenty years, and he didn't make my instincts sit up and wiggle their ears. He was an anomaly. It was a crime of passion, after all, and they are hard to get a handle on. He probably didn't know himself that he was going to pull that trigger until he did pull it."

"Yeah, but I knew about his passion. I just didn't know how screwed up he actually was."

"No one ever knows, and no one knew – not his sister or his parents or his friends. Not even Rick himself, likely.

Not to change the subject – actually, I want to change the subject. Here." Jenkins reached into his pocket, took out a small box and pushed it across the table.

"What's this?" Delmont opened the lid. Inside was a ring. A silver ring engraved with two hands clasped around a heart wearing a crown.

Jenkins spoke to the table. "It's an Irish ring, a Claddagh ring. I got it in one of the many shops on this street that sell Irish kitsch. They go back a long way, these kind of rings, right back to the Romans."

"The Romans were Irish? Gee, you learn something new every day."

"You're a funny girl. No, the Romans weren't Irish, but these rings – they signify faith and loyalty and friendship and have a long European history. Or so the girl in the shop told me."

"Some cop you are, believing what an Irish shopgirl who probably swallowed the Blarney Stone tells you. What else did she say?" My God thought Delmont, he's blushing. She felt a ripple of fear combined with something that was possibly delight.

Jenkins stopped looking at the table and stared straight into her eyes. "She said there's a bunch of different ways you can wear it. For example, if you're married, you wear it on the ring finger of your left hand, with the point of the heart towards your wrist. If you wear it on the right hand with the point toward your fingertips, you're single. And if you wear it on your right hand with the point towards the wrist, well, it means someone has captured your heart."

"I see." Delmont did see, clearly for once. She took the ring out of the box and held it up to the light. It shone like a little moon. And then she pulled it on over the ring finger of her right hand. With the point of the heart towards her wrist. She looked at Jenkins and knew she would be flying out tomorrow.

Because his face was so bright that the fog didn't stand a chance.

Afterword

On July 1st, 1992, The Town of Bay Bulls was celebrating
Canada Day. The Fisheries patrol vessel Leonard J. Cowley
was tied to the public wharf in my hometown for this
celebration. John Crosbie, Member of Parliament for St.
John's West and Federal Fisheries Minister was scheduled to
speak from the deck of this vessel for the celebration. My
father, Mike Ryan, one of the staunchest conservatives in the
riding of St. John's West, was Mayor at the time. Minister
Crosbie and his wife Jane attended my father's house before
this gathering. Crosbie rarely drove down the Southern Shore
without dropping in for a political chat with my father.
Sometimes these chats were enjoyed over a cup of tea, coffee
or a stiff drink. On the morning in question. I was on the wharf
assisting with setting up the sound system for this event.

All of a sudden, hundreds of burly fishermen started

arriving. I quickly put two and two together and realized what was happening or about to happen. These fishermen weren't there to celebrate Canada's 125th birthday, but to take out their frustration on the Federal Fisheries Minister. I owned a convenience store nearby at the time. I quickly drove back to my store and called the RCMP in Ferryland and explained what was about to transpire. They said they would send an officer, but it would be at least a half-hour before they would arrive.

I went to my father's residence to inform Mr. Crosbie of what was on the go.

I walked in and said: "Excuse me, Minister Crosbie we have a problem, there are hundreds of fishermen on the public wharf awaiting your arrival and more arriving as we speak. I have called the RCMP in Ferryland for security, I was told it will take them at least a half-hour before arriving. You should wait for them to arrive, before going to the wharf."

With that, Mr. Crosbie stood up from the couch, as did my father who was sitting next to Mr. Crosbie. Mr. Crosbie elbowed my father in the ribs and said: "Come on Mike, let's not keep them waiting."

I followed Mr. and Mrs. Crosbie along with my father to the public wharf. Mr. Crosbie got out of his vehicle, he never blinked and walked headfirst into the crowd of angry fishermen.

It was a dismal morning weather-wise, as were the faces of

the fishermen. I honestly thought that morning, the scavenging seagulls would carry the last of the Minister away.

July 1st, 1992, was the day the Moratorium on Northern Cod came into effect. Throwing forty-thousand Newfoundland fish plant workers, fishermen and fisherwomen out of work. It was the biggest layoff in Canadian history. Up to the writing and publication of this book, the Northern Cod stock is but a shadow of what it was pre-1992.

That night, July 1, 1992, my father, and I watched John Crosbie, the federal fisheries minister, announce a moratorium on the Northern Cod fishery in Newfoundland on the CBC National news. The news broadcast showed Crosbie being verbally accosted on the public wharf in Bay Bulls by hundreds of angry and furious fishermen.

After the coverage of the moratorium ended, my father looked at me and said, "We're paying for those baby bonus checks now." I thought that was one of the best Newfoundland political quotes I had ever heard. And I've been an astute political observer since my preteen years.

The following month the Federal Government announced a federal aid program call Northern Cod Adjustment and Recovery Program {NCARP}. This program was to supplement and retrain fish plant workers, fishermen and fisherwomen until the cod stocks recovered.

Acknowledgments

Thank you to my editor Susan Rendell and my copy editor Tamara Church.

Lorna Yard - Cover Designer.

Book cover photograph, "Red Cliff." "Ray Mackey Photography."

An extra special thank you to my talented step-daughter Stacie Wakeham. Stacie keeps me on the straight and narrow with technology/computers. I'm a very slow learner. I always say I should have been born a hundred years earlier than 1964 when it comes to technology such as computers, cell phones and smart televisions.

My wife, Tina Wakeham Ryan. Who has great patience with me and knows all my characters almost as well as myself before passing them out to the world and letting them run wild. Love You!

My proofreaders before editing for finding my mistakes and errors and for their positive critiquing and constructive advice. Ron Fahey, Adam Hodder, Perry Howlett and Wanda Ronayne.

People ask why I use so many proofreaders. I consider myself a storyteller, not a writer. It takes many people and different sets of eyes to turn my ramblings into a legible document. Without these people, my stories would never see a library bookshelf. People also ask what I want to achieve with my writing. If a few dozen people tell me they enjoyed my most recent book, I'm happy. I've changed my hobby from being a voracious reader to being a prolific writer.

I credit Tina with me becoming a writer. About a year after the now infamous 2010 *Bay Bulls Standoff*, I started saying to my wife, "I wish someone would write a book about the standoff." I knew there was a good story/book there. After saying this many times, she said; "Shut up, and go write the damn book." The next day I wrote thirty-five hundred and as the saying goes...the rest is history.

A big thank you to my loyal readers who enjoy my writings.

If you read my books. Please leave a review on Amazon.ca/Amazon.com or Goodreads.com. Reviews help so much. Thank you.

I can be reached at chrisryan64@hotmail.com

About the Author

Christopher P Ryan was born on March 6th, 1964, the eighth in a family of nine children. His family has operated Ryan's Funeral Home in Bay Bulls, serving the Southern Shore for over fifty years.

Twice elected to the town council for his hometown of Bay Bulls, first in 1993 and 1997. He also sat on the board of directors for the East Coast Trail Association for five years, serving the last year as vice-president. On April 23, 2013, he was awarded the Flamber Head Award for volunteerism for years of service on the lobbying committee and the first project management committee of this group and its board of directors.

Chris spent several years on the Ferryland District Liberal Association and served the last two years as president. A former board member of Say No to American Garbage Group

(SNAGG), an organization that opposed the importation of garbage/waste into Newfoundland and Labrador for final distribution. He is a former member of the Witless Bay and Area Conservation Group. This group's goal is to protect sea trout and salmon that visit the Lower Pond in Witless Bay. A pond made world-famous for record-sized sea-run brown trout.

On August 21/2019, Chris was awarded the Sovereign's Medal for Volunteering with the East Coast Trail Association for 25 years. Chris is a serious birder who has seen 342 species of birds in Newfoundland. He holds a second-degree black belt in Shotokan Traditional Karate from the Newfoundland Karate Association.

Chris is a provincially ranked 8 and 9 ball pool player. Who has travelled to Las Vegas to represent the province in billiards.